NIGHTMARES OF A
HUSTLA 2

King Dream

**Lock Down Publications and Ca$h
Presents
NIGHTMARES OF A HUSTLA 2
A Novel by *King Dream***

King Dream

Lock Down Publications
P.O. Box 944
Stockbridge, Ga 30281

Visit our website @
www.lockdownpublications.com

Copyright 2020 King Dream
NIGHTMARES OF A HUSTLA 2

Lock Down Publications
Like our page on Facebook: Lock Down Publications @
www.facebook.com/lockdownpublications.ldp
Cover design and layout by: **Dynasty Cover Me**
Book interior design by: **Shawn Walker**
Edited by**: Shamika Smith**

Stay Connected with Us!

Text **LOCKDOWN** to 22828 to stay up-to-date with new releases, sneak peaks, contests and more...
Thank you.

Submission Guideline.

Submit the first three chapters of your completed manuscript to ldpsubmissions@gmail.com, subject line: Your book's title. The manuscript must be in a .doc file and sent as an attachment. Document should be in Times New Roman, double spaced and in size 12 font. Also, provide your synopsis and full contact information. If sending multiple submissions, they must each be in a separate email.

Have a story but no way to send it electronically? You can still submit to LDP/Ca$h Presents. Send in the first three chapters, written or typed, of your completed manuscript to:

LDP: Submissions Dept
P.O. Box 944
Stockbridge, Ga 30281

DO NOT send original manuscript. Must be a duplicate.

Provide your synopsis and a cover letter containing your full contact information.

Thanks for considering LDP and Ca$h Presents.

Dedicated to James Stewart

King Dream

Chapter 1

Lil Wayne's song, "Darkside", plays through the speaker as King Nut pulls up in front of Williams Holmes Borders Apartments in his black Hummer truck. He gets out and walks up the steps that led to the apartment building. His long, purple dreadlocks with gold tips swayed from side to side as he swaggered through the apartment complex. A group of eight niggas shot dice in a gated off circle that was originally designed as a barbeque pit area. Two crackheads sat on one of the staircases drinking cans of 211. Raw sewage could be seen overflowing and flowing underneath the gutter grates.

King Nut went down a few stairs and went to apartment number six. Two little niggas sat posted on crates with 40 Glocks on their waste. Both of them stand up to greet King Nut and he shakes up with them before knocking on the door. A kid around the age of eleven answered the door with a Tec-9 strapped around his neck and his finger on the trigger. "Wassup, King Nut?"

"Wassup, Lil Yogi? You holding it down in here, lil nigga?" King Nut says as he walked into the house.

"You know it," Lil Yogi says locking the door back. A Jamaican man stood in the roach-infested kitchen. He stood over the stove with a Pyrex in a pot of water whipping up some work. A teenage boy around sixteen stood next to him learning the art of how to cook up dope.

"K-Roc, what it do?" he says, putting his hand on his right-hand man's shoulder. K-Roc was also his brother-in-law. King Nut was married to his sister, La'dee. K-Roc and La'dee were raised in Kingston, Jamaica. King Nut has known them since they all were kids. He was born and raised in Jamaica too. He and his mama moved to

Atlanta when he was fourteen. He and La'dee had always been in love. A few years after he came to Atlanta, he started hustling to stack money to move her and K-Roc there with him. He accomplished that in a matter of two months, but the money was so good that he couldn't stop hustling. And eventually, he and K-Roc begin to take over the Atlanta metro area.

"Maybe you should really think about mending things

between you and Billy Gunz. I'm tired of this bullshit work, mon. Ever since you stopped fucking with him, our dope has been pure bullshit you know." King Nut lifts up a paper towel to see what was covered under the plate. When he opens it, he sees a group of roaches feasting on a grilled cheese sandwich. He pushed the plate away.

"Fuck a Billy Gunz. He wants to play God in this game. He thinks he could take Atlanta from me and make me one of his mini kingpins. No! No one is above King Nut, you dig?" he says, poking himself in the chest with his finger.

"Then you better think about finding another plug because this dope has been stepped on more than Rodney King," he says stirring the water with his hand by shaking the glass. Then looking at the small amount of oil that rose to the top.

"No worries. We'll find a better connect, my nigga. Just be patient. Rome wasn't built overnight. And call an exterminator before these roaches run off with all our dope," he says stumping on a few roaches. K-Roc waves him off and begins dropping ice cubes into the water.

King Nut then walks to the back room. Another little soldier sat posted in a chair by the door with a Tec-9 in his lap while he texted on the phone. His bitch had just sent him a pic with her ass in the air and he was all smiles. When the lil nigga sees King Nut approaching, he puts his phone away and gets up to unlocks the door for him.

King Nut walks inside and locks the door behind him. The room had a bedroom set and a television along with some other room décor. It all was just a decoy. He walks over and removes the false plug outlet behind the bed. Behind the outlet was a keypad. He punches in his four-digit pin code and part of the wall slid open revealing a safe. He punches in another pin number and collects the money out of the safe before leaving.

His money had been getting lighter and lighter since cutting ties with Billy Gunz. He hadn't been able to catch a decent plug with good work since. His hustle was suffering terribly, and Billy Gunz controlled all the good work in the whole United States. But getting back right with Billy Gunz meant giving up the throne of Atlanta to incorporate it with the Black Order, which is something King Nut refuses to do. And because of that, Billy Gunz had been starving him and his crew by not supplying them with any decent work. Billy Gunz knew one way or another, King Nut would have to either bow down or die out. King Nut was determined to survive and continue to reign as King of Atlanta by any means necessary.

He jumped into his Hummer and drove off from the apartment building. He pulled into the parking lot of a community college twenty minutes away from the apartments. He rolls up a blunt of sour diesel laced with cocaine inside a Backwood cigar while he waits for La'dee to get out of class. She was going to school to pursue her dreams of being one of Atlanta's most successful high-end realtors.

He checks the time, and it reads 2:20 PM. He had ten minutes before class let out. Enough time to blow a blunt and catch the high he needed. He had just caught a ball of coke to try out from a potential new plug.

He sparks up the blunt and leans back in his seat. Concealed behind the tint on his windows, he inhales the smoke from the laced blunt. Sweat starts to run down his face, but he refused to roll down the windows or turn the air-conditioning on. He didn't want any of the smoke escaping.

He turns on the radio and Kardinal Offishall's song, "Lighters!", plays. He needed this moment to ease his mind. So much stress trying to maintain his throne in Atlanta, drove him to smoking primos to keep his mind tamed. No one knew about his little habit; not even La'dee or K-Roc. All he could think about is finding a steady plug so all his problems would be erased. Everyone in the nearby states were under Billy Gunz's organization or had bullshit dope.

The school doors opened, taking him out of his thoughts. He quickly put the remainder of the blunt out and hid it in his sun visor. He sprayed air freshener and rolled the windows down. The breeze coming through the window felt good to him as it cooled his skin.

The students began filing out of the school building. A strapped caramel skin woman with green eyes walks over to the truck and opens the passenger door. She gets in and puts her Gucci backpack in the backseat.

"Hey baby," she says as she leans over and gives him a kiss.

"Wassup, baby? How was class?" he asks as he backs out of his parking space.

"It was good. We learned about all the different forms of mortgages and financing," she says as she pulls a blunt out of her purse and sparks it up.

"You sound excited." She passes him the blunt. He takes a hard pull and holds the smoke in a moment before letting it out.

"I am. In just a few more months, I will be a certified

realtor mon," she says with much excitement. Like King Nut when she came to the states she learned how to talk like the locals. But their Jamaican accents came out strong when they were mad or overly excited.

As she went on about how hard she's been working and how happy she was to be so close to graduating, King Nut began to feel funny. His eyelids felt heavy and his heart was beating faster than he had ever felt. He started sweating profusely.

La'dee stops talking when she hears his breathing starts to become rapid. She looks over at him. His face was soaked in sweat and his eyes were starting to roll in the back of his head. "Nut!! What's wrong!" Nut fell back into his seat unconscious. La'dee quickly grabs the wheel but not before the truck hit the curve. She quickly turned the steering wheel to the left to avoid a crowd of people. But when she turned the truck ran right into the side of an ambulance. La'dee hit her head on the dashboard and fell unconscious too.

When King Nut came to, he was lying in the hospital bed cuffed to its railing. His head was bandaged, and his arm was in a cask. La'dee was getting up from a chair nearby and walking over to him. "Baby, are you okay?" she asked, rubbing his hand.

"What happened?" His voice was groggy and dry.

"You lost consciousness and we had an accident. The doctors said you had weed and coke with a mix of horse tranquilizers in your system. They said you could've died if the EMT's hadn't been there to help. What was coke and horse tranquilizers doing in your system Nut? And don't lie to me." She holds a cup in front of him and puts the straw to his lips. He takes a few sips.

"Somebody must've mixed some in the coke I tried out from a new connect."

"You doing coke now?"

"No! I just had to taste it to see if the shit was real. I'll tell you one thing, that nigga's a dead man when I get out of this damn hospital. And why the fuck am I in these cuffs?" he asked, trying to raise his cuffed hand.

"Because you were under the influence when the accident happened. The doctors found coke, both soft and crack, in your boxers when they removed your clothes. They handed it over to the police and now they're charging you with it."

"Next case is in the matter of the State versus Nuthell Henry. Charges of driving under the influence of illegal drugs, two counts possession of illegal substances, and two counts of endangering public safety." King Nut sat in front of the judge and awaited his fate. With the dope stashed by his nut sack and him being passed out in the driver's seat, they had him dead to rights with no way out.

"How does the defendant plead?" the judge asked.

"Guilty, your honor," Attorney Daniel Winehouse says on King Nut's behalf.

"Is that to all counts?"

"Yes, your honor," King Nut confirms. "What is prosecution recommending?"

"Your honor, the State is requesting that Mr. Henry does three years of incarceration and a year probation. The defendant has a rap sheet consisting of prior drug possession and one count of home invasion."

"All in which Mr. Henry was acquitted," Attorney Winehouse interjects. The judge taps his fingers on the bench as he looks at King Nut with a stern face. "Your honor, my client -" The judge holds up his hand cutting him off.

"I've heard enough counsel. I have my decision ready. Mr. Henry, rise while I read you your fate." King Nut and his lawyer got to their feet. When the judge read off his punishment, he couldn't believe the sentence that was handed down to him.

King Dream

Chapter 2

"Hi, my name is Daryl and I'm an addict. I've been addicted to meth for the past three years..." the man goes on about his life story. King Nut sat in a chair in the circle with his arms folded across his chest. The place was as luxurious as any rehab facility he'd ever seen. They catered to the rich and famous. There was every amenity available you could think of to pamper the most pampered celebrity or rich person. But King Nut could think of a million and one other things he could be doing right then instead of being there. However, he had no choice but to be there by orders of the court. It was the only way to get out of a dope case he was facing. It was either go to rehab or go to jail.

When the meeting ended everyone left out the meeting room. On the way to his room, he passed by the game room. When he passed by, he saw a man passing a known pop singer a small zip lock bag with white powder under the card table. The woman then passed him a roll of bills.

King Nut walks into the game room and takes a seat at a nearby table where Jinx sat. Jinx was a rich white boy that King Nut met when he first got to the rehab facility. "Jinx, who's the new stud over there," Nut asked him, pointing his head at the man that just dealt to the pop singer.

"Oh him? That's Pay Pay. He checks in every few months to deal drugs to the residents," he says while shuffling a deck of cards. Then he leans in closer to Nut and whispers to him. "And he has some of the best coke I've ever put up my nose."

"Really?"

"Really," Jinx tells him with a serious face and tone. Nut watches Pay Pay for a minute then slides Jinx a hundred.

"Grab us a taste of it." Jinx takes the money.

"Wait 'til his next game starts, and I'll go over there and get some."

"Why wait when you could just go over there right now and get some?" Jinx deals the cards out between him and King Nut.

"You got to wait for your turn to play if you want to make a purchase. That's just how he handles business. He's a real stickler about following his rules of doing business."

The game ended and Jinx walked over to Pay Pay's table to play. King Nut watched how smoothly Pay Pay moved when he made his exchanges. He passed the dope to whoever sat next to him and they passed it down to the intended person and the money came back the same way. That way everybody was guilty of the drug transaction if ever caught.

When the game ended Jinx got up and signaled King Nut with his head to follow him. King Nut follows him to his room.

King Nut closes the door behind him, and Jinx poured the powder out onto a plate. He takes a card out of the deck and makes eight thin lines of powder. He rolls up a hundred-dollar bill and begins vacuuming up four of the lines before passing the straw to King Nut. Nut takes the straw and blows a line. The potency of the powder took him by surprise. He had gotten used to the heavily stepped on dope he's been having to settle for lately. And the powder he just tooted was so powerful he caught an instant high off one thin line of it. He pinches his nose, and it begins to run immediately. "Damn, this is some good shit," he says before blowing another line.

"What I tell you, man? Dude has the best shit I ever had," Jinx says as he turns up the music and Linkin Park's song, "I'll Be Gone", blares through the speakers on his iPod dock.

"You think he'll be down to sell some heavy weight of this shit to me?"

"I don't know man. Pay Pay is a real careful kind of guy. He don't too much fuck with people who ain't well known or who he don't know much about."

"What the fuck does he know about you? You ain't well known. Yo daddy just got that Wall Street money, nothing special. So why he fuck with you?"

"It took a lot for me to get in the door, trust me. This guy did a full background check on me and my family before he even spoke to me."

"For dope this good, I don't give a fuck if he did background checks on my whole family tree. Just get me in the door," he says passing Jinx the plate.

"Alright, I'll give him your name and everything. But I'm not making any promises," he says loading the plate up with another eight lines.

"Just make it do what it do."

******

It's been a week since Jinx gave Pay Pay King Nut's info and he still hadn't heard anything back. His patience was running thin. He needed to get his hands on some better work for his spots on the outs before he loses everything. He walks into the entertainment room and sits down at the table with Jinx.

"What's up, Nut?"

"Look you said it took him four days to get back to you after he did a background check on you. It's been a whole week and yo mans still haven't got back with me. I need you to go holla at him and see what's up."

"I can't. I told you this guy is real strict about how he

conducts business. If I go over there sweating him about you, he's going to think we're on some police shit and stop doing business with me. No offense my friend, you're cool and all, but not worth losing a contact that good. Just chill, he'll get back to you." King Nut wasn't trying to hear any of that. That nigga, Pay Pay, was stalling him and he had to see why. As soon as the game ended, he got up and headed over to the table. "Nut, what are you doing?" King Nut ignored him and went over and snatched up a seat at the table before the person it was reserved for could sit down.

"Hey, I had winners."

"Not today mothafucka. Move around."

"You know it's kind of rude to take someone's seat," Pay Pay says shuffling a deck of cards.

"Yeah well, it's also rude to stall someone out for a whole week straight. Now I'm trying to do business with you."

"Business? I don't know what you talking about. I have no business here other than receiving the treatment I need to overcome my addiction. Now if you don't mind me and my friends would like to get our game started." King Nut mugged Pay Pay for a second then got up and went back over the table where Jinx sat.

"What he say?"

"He played dumb." Jinx shook his head at him. "I told you not to go over there."

"Jinx!" Pay Pay called from his table. "What's up, Pay Pay?"

"Your friend is skinny as fuck. He needs to work out more. Pushing weight takes strength," Pay Pay says and holds up the ten of diamonds for Jinx to see. "I think I might have them on this hand."

"I know what you mean. I'll make sure he works out

more. In fact, I'm going to get him in the gym tonight." Pay Pay nods his head.

Jinx turns to King Nut and whispers to him. "Dude, you lucky bastard. He wants you to meet him in the gym at ten tonight."

"I'll be there."

It is ten o'clock on the dot when King Nut walks into the gym. With exception of the two women on the treadmills and a man on a stationary bike, the gym was empty. He easily spots Pay Pay on the bench press. He walks over to him. "I see you are one of those real cautious type of nigga." Pay Pay lifts the weights for two more reps then sits them back on the bar stand. He dusts his hands off while sitting up.

"They say caution is for the wise. And action without thought is for the foolish. Now, how can I help you?"

"My boy, Jinx, gave me a taste of some of this cake he had, and I want to get my hands on a lot more of it. So, I come to holla at the baker and see what's good." King Nut sits on the butterfly press and starts working out.

"Okay then, the baker's answer is no." "What you mean no?"

"Meaning I did my research on you. Nuthell Henry, you're from Kingston, Jamaica. You're twenty-nine years old. You had a few dismissed cases for drug possession and a recent case for a home invasion that you beat just last year due to the fact that the two witnesses came up missing. All cases were handled by the attorney, Daniel Winehouse, the best attorney in all of Georgia. So that let me know you weren't a snitch or a cop."

"So, what's the problem?"

"The problem is the person that I get my work from got you on the starve list. He forbids anyone to sell any weight of his work in Atlanta."

21

"Billy Gunz. Damn!" he says, letting the weight slam down and causing everybody in the room to look his way.

"Now if you're done drawing attention to us, I would like to continue my workout."

"Wait a minute. If you weren't going to do business with me, then you would've told me that as soon as you got the info back on me. But you didn't. Instead, you had me meet you here. You were thinking about doing it anyway. Weren't you?"

"I was considering it, but it's too risky. Now I don't know what the beef is between you and Billy Gunz, but that doesn't have shit to do with me. I heard you got Atlanta on lock. And because of that, I would love to do business with you. If I get caught serving to you after Billy Gunz puts you on the starve list, then I will be on the same diet as you if not dead."

"Who says he has to know?"

"I know you ain't that stupid. Billy Gunz got eyes everywhere and knows everything."

"Listen Pay Pay, we can both stand to make a lot of money doing business together. You don't even have to go through me directly. We can use the white boy Jinx to work as a go-between." King Nut could see the wheels inside of Pay Pay's head turning.

"If I'm going to put myself at risk of losing my connection with Billy Gunz and face certain death by dealing with you, you're going to have to do me a favor."

"What sort of favor?"

"I need some niggas pushed out the game."

"Who you need gone?"

"Big Country and Popeye."

"Big Country and Popeye? Me have no problem with them. Dem hustle but dem respect me as the King of Atlanta.

Dem boyz even buy from me sometimes. They like brothas to me."

"Maybe so. But them brothas are the ones that stand in the way of us doing business. They are a problem for me. They know people in Billy Gunz circle who are more than willing to report to Billy Gunz himself for a chance to get connected. Too much of a risk for me. Get rid of them and we can do business."

"I don't know mon. Let me think on it."

"You got twenty-four hours before this offer expires. So, if I was you, I would think fast," Pay Pay says, leaving the gym room.

******

King Nut calls K-Roc to get an update on what's been going on. "Yeah mon."

"K-Roc. Wassup my nigga?"

"Not this work. This shit is killing business. You got people switching to dealing meth because there's no good dope in the city, mon."

"I'm working on something now, brah. Did you find them niggas that sold me the bullshit that got me in here?"

"No. Dem boys started laying low once the streets told them who you were. But I'm sure we'll find them soon."

"Aight, keep hustling that shit off we got and I'm going keep trying to work on getting this plug into selling to me."

"Aight, one." K-Roc ends the call. King Nut had no other choice. He had to scratch a deal with Pay Pay before he lost his crown in the streets.

He went searching for Pay Pay and finds him relaxing in a lawn chair near the pool, reading a book. "You got a deal, mon. I'll take care of Popeye and Big Country before the month is over with," he says as he takes the empty seat next to him.

"Nah, you go home in two days, and in two days is the start of a fresh week. So, you got only one week to have that problem solved or that deals off the table, brah," Pay Pay says while not taking his eyes off the book in his hand.

"One week? Are you mad, mon? You want me to off one of Atlanta's biggest dealers and his general enforcer, who are me friends, in just one week?"

"That shouldn't be too hard for the King of Atlanta to do. If it is, then I guess you're not really the king and I'm wasting my time conversing with you."

"Wait it a minute, mon. I am the only King of Atlanta. Don't you dare even verbally try to take me crown. You say one week. Then if I do this, I want to get me kilos from you at thirty a key and not a penny more."

"Nope, not good enough."

"What do you mean not good enough?" King Nut was starting to get agitated with Pay Pay. He was a hard person to bargain with. King Nut was used to getting his way with anybody he came across. But like Billy Gunz, Pay Pay had to have things his way or no way at all. He had the leverage to have it that way and that pissed King Nut off because he knew he had no choice but to bow down to him.

"Meaning I'll do you better than that. I'll give them to you for twenty-five a key. So, do we have a deal or what?" King Nut wasn't expecting that answer. It was a better deal than he could ever bargain for.

"Twenty-five a key? Dem boys will be dead before the end of the week."

"Then the Sunday after next you'll be flooding the city with the best work around."

King Nut might've been the King of Atlanta, but Big

Country was nobody to fuck over either. Big Country was a gangsta originally from the Chi and well connected with some serious names back in his city. Popeye was just as gangsta and was Big Country's General Enforcer. He ran all of Big Country's spots. King Nut knew it was going to be some strong repercussions behind making such hits. But for the price on their heads, he was more than willing to make it happen.

King Dream

Chapter 3

Fresh out of rehab, King Nut had something else he's been longing for. He unlocks the door with his key and enters the house. He unzips his pants and pulls out his member as the thick chocolate woman comes into the front room.

"Wow, not even a 'hello, Karen. How are you', first?"

"We don't have much time before Lil Nut gets home from school and La'dee gets to hounding me."

"She doesn't know that Lil Nut catches the bus home from school?"

"You think I'll be here if she did? You know that crazy bitch would pull up over here and kill us both."

"How you know I didn't have a man or company or something before you came in here whipping yo dick out like that?"

"I wouldn't give a fuck. That nigga would just have to be mad. You know that pussy belongs to me anyway. Anytime I pull this mothafucka out, you know what time it is, and you better get down to business. Now, are you going to keep wasting our quality time with all this talking or are we going to bust these nuts?" Without another word to be said, she goes down on him and his head falls back on the couch. She caresses his member with her luscious lips, and he releases sounds of verbal excitement.

"I don't see why you are with her instead of me anyway," she says while giving him some head.

"Karen, stop talking with your mouth full. That's very unladylike." She rolls her eyes and shuts up as she goes back to work on him. Moments later, she straddles him and his hands roam across her thick chocolate ass cheeks. As he enters her, she moans softly, winding her hips and grinding on him. He digs deep inside of her until they both found ecstasy.

******

His phone rings, taking him out of a conversation with Karen and Lil Nut. He shuts her up before answering it. "Yes, it's me, love."

"Nut, what are you doing?"

"It's 3:40, what do you think I'm doing?" he says, sparking his blunt from earlier back up and blowing out a cloud of smoke.

"Exactly, it's 3:40. Lil Nut gets out of school at 2:30. It only takes twenty-three minutes to get him home. That's forty-seven minutes you've been over that bitch's house doing only God knows what." King Nut rubs his head and exhales a heavy breath.

"Damn La'dee, stop with the jealousy and insecurity bullshit. I was spending some time with me boy."

"That better be the only one you spend time with over there. I will be smelling your dick when you come home, you hear me?"

"Is that all you called me for La'dee? I got better things to do right now than to argue with you." La'dee had never let King Nut live down the fact he cheated on her and got another woman pregnant. She knew he messed around with other women, but having a kid with another woman went too far for her. They broke up for a few months and got back together. She loved Lil Nut, but she and Karen couldn't stand each other.

"No, I was calling to tell you K-Roc's been trying to get a hold of you. He says he found dem boys you been looking for and he wants you to meet up with him at the club."

"I'm on my way." He ended the call and put his phone

away. When he stood up to leave, Karen grabbed him by the arm.

"Where you going so fast?"

"I'ma holla at you later this week. I got some business to take care of."

"Now ain't that some shit. She snaps her fingers and you go running." Karen crossed her legs and folded her arms across her chest giving him attitude.

"I don't have time for your reverse psychology bullshit. Me leaving right now has nothing to do with going to spend time with La'dee. I told you, I got business to take care of." He bent down and planted a kiss on her forehead. "I'll see you later." He left out the door leaving Karen fuming in her jealousy. All he could think was *bitches are something else.*

******

King Nut and La'dee walked into a private room in the back of Club Jam Rock. This was a nightclub King Nut owned in the College Park area.

Inside the private room, two men sat back to back tied down to their chairs. King Nut's men form a circle around the two men. King Nut walks slowly in circles around the men tied to the chairs with his hands behind his back as he speaks. "You come in me ghetto and hustle yo dummy drugs to me clientele. Getting em sick and getting me sick!"

"King Nut, I'm sorry. Man, my bad. We was just trying to get some quick cash so we could get back on our feet," one of the men tells him.

"Yeah, we didn't mean for nobody to get hurt. We swear," the other man says.

"No, no, the damage has been done, mon. Me customers keep me rich and keep me wife looking good. When someone comes in me hood and hustles, they take money out me mouth, me son's mouth, and out of me wife's mouth." He points to La'dee. "And like the Snickers' commercial, when we're hungry, we're not ourselves. It makes me crazy, you know? And when I'm crazy, she's crazy and me boy is just as crazy."

"Come on King Nut. We didn't even know that was your turf. If we would've known that we would've never been over there. We wouldn't dare step on your toes. Come on, I know we can work something out."

"How do you not know? All of Atlanta belongs to me, mon. But you want to work something out? Okay, we can work something out." King Nut looks over at one of his men. "Bring the tray." The man nods his head and walks into another room. A few seconds later, he returns with a tray with some lighters, rocks, and crack pipes on it. "You want to make things right then it's only fair, mon, that you take in what you dished out. Here, I made my own dummy rocks for the two of you. If we're going to make things right, then the two of you are going to smoke these rocks until the quarter ounce of it is gone. You hear me?" They both nod their heads in agreement. "K-Roc untie them." K-Roc orders two men to untie the men.

The men load up their pipes with the rocks and begin to smoke. They were expecting to inhale candle wax or something of the sort. To their surprise, they immediately began to tweak.

"What is in this?" one of the men asks, choking. King Nut laughs.

"A lil of this and a lil of that. Some meth, crack, heroin, and a few other things. Back in Jamaica, we call it a Crunch Bar. We used it to get people hooked. It's very addictive. So now you bitch ass niggas will be some hypes." The men sweated and began to space out. King Nut turns to K-Roc. "How is business going on?"

"Business is not so good, mon. Our customers are so thirsty for better dope that they're constantly spending their money with every new dealer that they come across. That's why they keep getting played by bombaclaats like them," K-Roc says, pointing his head at the two men smoking the Crunch Bars.

"Don't worry, brah. I'm working on something right now."

"You say that all the time, mon. But me customers aren't trying to hear it anymore. Dem want to get high and this shit is not getting them there. So, whatever you're working on better work out fast."

"It will mon, it will. In fact, get some soldiers together this week because we got a couple of moves to make. We do this and we'll be back in business." One of the men smoking falls out of the chair and hits the floor passing out. A second later, the other man does the same.

"Maybe I should've told them to pace themselves," King Nut says with a laugh.

******

Popeye, the Puerto Rican drug dealer on the South Side, sat on the couch inside the spot watching an episode of "Atlanta's Housewives". A couple of his soldiers sat around watching too. On the show, Cardi Red walks into the restaurant and the camera gets a nice shot of her ass before she takes a seat. The whole house yell, "Damn."

"God damnnn! I swear that bitch got a fat ass on her. I ain't even gon lie. I'll pay for some of that there," Oreo said.

"Nigga please, you ain't even got enough money to pay

for that pussy. That hoe's shoes cost more than you could afford to pay, you half-bred bastard," Lil Dee tells him.

"And whatever I lack in paper, I can make up for with game. After I game that bitch and hit the pussy, she'll be trying to pay me. Real talk."

"And you'll never get that chance to see if that's true. Because you don't ever see these hoes on this show in the city and probably never will. Now shut the fuck up and watch the damn show," Purp tells them.

"I bet a hunnid this bitch splash that drink in that hoe's face," Popeye says.

"What I look like, stupid? Everybody knows whenever these bitches on reality shows argue and there are drinks around, them drinks getting tossed in each other's faces. You won't be getting an easy hunnid out of me. Trick no good, my nigga." Moments later on the show, drinks got to flying and the women started fighting.

"Ooh wee, get that bitch!" Popeye yells at the TV. Somebody knocks at the backdoor. Everybody was deep off into the fight on TV watching for pussy and ass shots or a titty to pop out, even though they knew it would be censored.

"Oreo, get the door," Purp says.

"Man, why don't you make Lil Dee get the door? I'm trying to see these hoes get down."

"Cuz I told yo White, monkey looking ass to get it. Now get yo ass up and get the door."

"Man!" Oreo says smacking his lips and getting up. He walks through the kitchen to the back door. "Who is it?"

"It's Tit Ball, baby. Let me get three of em." As soon as Oreo opens the door, K-Roc pushes Tit Ball out the way. As soon as he did that, he busts off one shot from the Street Sweeper, hitting Oreo in the chest. The blast sent him flying across the kitchen and hitting the wall, then falling to the floor dead. Three soldiers walk in behind K-Roc with Dracos in hand.

Popeye and his boys hear the shots and pull out their heat. Popeye grabs the chopper from under the couch. Lil Dee walks towards the kitchen with the 9mm in hand. He fires a couple of shots at one of the soldiers coming through the door but misses. The lil soldier squeezes off a barrage of shots Lil Dee's way, making him take cover.

Purp pops off a few shots in K-Roc's direction and then Popeye sends a stream of shots into the kitchen. K-Roc's men started busting their way towards the living room. Lil Dee bust off three quick shots, catching one of K-Roc's lil soldiers in the shoulder. The lil nigga was so gone off Mollies and Perks that he didn't even flinch when the bullet hit him. Instead, he quickly steadied his aim like K-Roc had taught him and sent two shots to Lil Dee's face, dropping him instantly. "Good shot, boy!" K-Roc tells his lil soldier.

Popeye squeezed off two shots just before a shell got jammed in the ejection slot. He tried to quickly get it unjammed, but it wasn't working. He tosses the riffle down and pulls out his .44 Magnum.

"Purp, we've got to go, brah. Let's bust our way out the front door," he says, hitting the remote starter on his Tahoe truck.

They both fired shots as they stayed low and made their way to the front door. Bullets soared passed their heads as they crawled to the door. "Purp, cover me while I get the door to unlock!" Popeye yells to him. They both get up. Purp fires shots as Popeye attacks the locks on the door. A rain of bullets riddled Purp's chest and he falls to the floor dead just as Popeye got the last lock unlocked. "Damn, Purp!" He opens the door, but before he could run off, he was facing down the barrel of a double barrel, .12-gauge, sawed-off shotgun.

"Sorry mon. I hate to be the bearer of bad news, but it's your time to go."

BOOM!

King Nut blows his head clean off his shoulders. "Make sure the lil soldiers take everything! They have three minutes!" he yells to K-Roc. And in exactly three minutes later, they were in the wind.

Chapter 4

La'dee and Audrey danced on the dance floor inside of Paradise Nightclub. Audrey was K-Roc's girl and her best friend. R. Kelly's song, "Slow Wine", played and La'dee was feeling herself. Her tight, turquoise, Fendi dress showed off her thick caramel legs and the curve of her big round booty. The way she was slowly grinding to the music had Big Country at his table with his hand on his crotch as he watched. He always wanted to see what La'dee's pussy was like. That ass of hers was so fat you had to be gay, dead, or blind not to want to hit that. But you also had to be a dumb mothafucka with a death wish to even attempt to try to hit it. Everyone knew La'dee belonged to King Nut and King Nut didn't play when it came to La'dee. Niggas that tried before, may they rest in peace. They found out the hard way why they call him King Nut.

La'dee looks over at Big Country, giving him a seductive smile and a wink. He couldn't help but smile back. She turns her ass in his direction so he could get a closer look as she danced. Her dress was so tight, he could see her thong print.

She leans over and whispers something in Audrey's ear just as the song plays out and another comes on. Audrey continued dancing and La'dee walked over to Big Country. "Big mon, you liked me dancing?"

"Hell yeah. Shit, dat there looked real good out there," he says looking at her ass.

"Oh, me don't know big mon. Me think me could've done better if me didn't have these clothes on. How would you like to see me dance for you in private?"

"I don't know about that shawty. Yo man finds out and shit could get real bad. But damn if that ass ain't tempting." She rubs her ass against his knee.

"Come on Big Country, I know you want me. Me want you too. And me won't tell me husband, if you won't."

"Is that right?" She grinds her ass a little harder on him. "It is so right, mon. So, how about we go to your car and have a little fun before I have to go home to him?" She whispers in his ear.

"Fuck it. Let's roll."

"Me had much to drink, mon. Let me go pee-pee first." La'dee goes to the bathroom. Minutes later, she was climbing on top of Big Country in the back of his Suburban truck. She grinds on top of him as she squeezes her small breast together.

"Damn baby, enough of this grinding, you got me there. Let me whip this big boi out and put it inside cha," he said, cuffing her ass cheeks in his hands.

"You got protection? We do nothing without it."

"Yeah, hold on." He opens the backdoor and goes to the front passenger's side door of the truck to get some rubbers out of the pocket of the door. He rushes back to the back of the truck, ready to wear La'dee's thick ass out. But when he gets back there, he sees the back of the truck was empty. La'dee was nowhere to be found. She had crept out while he wasn't looking. As soon as he turned around, King Nut was right there with the sawed-off.

"Damn, you tried to fuck my wife. Instead, you fucked yourself in the midst."

"Nigga, you done lost yo mind? You know you ain't getting away with this."

"I'm damn sho' gon' try."

BOOM!! BOOM!!

Big Country fell backwards into the back of his truck dead with two holes the size of saucer plates in his chest and stomach.

King Nut gets in his car with Audrey in the backseat and La'dee in the front and pulls off. "It took you long enough. Me text you ten minutes ago. Any longer and he would've been in me pum-pum!" La'dee tells him.

"And if that would've happened, trust me, you would've been just as dead as him." He pulls out his phone and dials Pay Pay's number. It goes straight to voicemail. "Damn!"

"What is it?"

"Pay Pay is not answering the phone."

"It's late, he's probably in bed. You know the major suppliers only work certain hours of the day. Stop acting brand new. Just call him tomorrow me king. You should be able to reach him then," she says, rubbing his head.

"Don't touch me, woman, 'til you shower. You smell like that fat mon," he said, pushing her hand away.

******

King Nut thought he had tied up all loose ends that lead to him being the one to hit Popeye and Big Country. But he had forgotten one.

Three crackheads sat on a rundown couch in a pissy ass parking lot next to a dumpster. Their torches lit up the night sky as they took blasts of their crack pipes. They share a bottle of Night Train between blasts. "Mannnn! I swear fo' God you wouldn't believe what I saw happen tonight."

"What you see, Tit Ball?" Otis asks him while taking a swig of the bottle of Night Train.

"I saw them niggas run up in Popeye's spot and kill everybody in there! I'm telling you it was blood and guts everywhere, mane."

"He lying his ass off again, Otis. That nigga tell mo tales than Aesop himself," Can-Man says before putting the torch to his crack pipe. They called him Can-Man because he was always asking people for cans to collect.

"Nigga, I ain't lying. If I'm lying, the lord in heaven could strike me down right now."

"You lying. And God won't strike you down because he wouldn't want to waste a lightning bolt on yo worthless black ass," Can-Man tells him.

"How else you think I got all this dope we smoking?

Dem niggas that did it hit my hand to not say nothing."

"That sounds like dey money went down the drain real quick," Can-Man says.

"If that's true, Tit Ball, then who did it?" Otis asked. "King Nut and his crew. They came in there and laid everybody down then took all dey shit."

"I told you that he's lying, Otis. That don't even make sense. Everybody knows King Nut supplies them and everybody else in Atlanta with their dope. So why would he rob and kill his own customer? Boi, I swear dey need to start putting surgeon general warning signs on crack bags because of dumb shit like this. It makes niggas like Tit Ball say the stupidest shit."

"Aight, you wait 'til the morning and you turn on the news. You'll see." They both wave Tit Ball off and continue smoking.

******

King Nut had just dropped Lil Nut off at his baby mama's house when he got the call. "Pay Pay, what it do brah?"

"You tell me."

"Did you see the tragedy on the news this morning? It seems two major drug dealers in Atlanta reaped the reaper's rewards last night."

"I've seen. It's a tragedy indeed, for some. For others, it's a blessing to have such men off the streets."

"Speaking of blessings, I have a hundred and fifty thousand ways to say I need to be blessed this beautiful Sunday morning."

"In that case, my wife will be meeting with yours this morning."

"For what? I handle me own business, mon, not me wife."

"Look here, Nut, since it's my ass on the line. If we going to do business, then we going to do it my way. Yo wife will have her instructions soon."

"But -" Pay Pay disconnected the call before King Nut could ask another question. "Bombaclaat!" he says, tossing the phone in the passenger seat.

La'dee steps out of her cranberry red Lexus coupe and puts on her Gucci shades. She felt uncomfortable and nowhere near sexy in the loose-fitting dress and stockings she was wearing, but it was what Noodles had instructed her to do. It was appropriate for where they were meeting that morning.

With a brand-new Gucci purse, that Noodles specifically told her to buy, in one hand and a Bible in the other, La'dee walks into the church. A man was singing a version of Marvin Sapp's song, "Never Would Have Made It", when she walked in. She takes a seat where Noodles had instructed her to sit and she waited.

La'dee wasn't into church and dreaded having to meet Noodles there. But to her surprise, she actually enjoyed some of the songs the choir sang. Just as she was getting into a song the choir was singing, one of the ushers walked up to her. "Excuse me, you the assistant Sunday school teacher, right?" he whispers to her.

"No, I'm sorry you're mistaken."

"Your name is Sister La'dee, right?"

"Yes, I'm La'dee."

"Then right this way. Sister Noodles is waiting for you," he says, stepping to the side holding his hand to point the way. La'dee gets up and follows the man back out into the lobby then down the hall to a classroom. The classroom was setup like a daycare filled with kids from five to eight years old. Dayla, Pay Pay and Noodles' daughter, sat in a swing set, napping while Noodles taught the kids the story of Noah and the ark.

Noodles sees La'dee and smiles. "Children, say hello to Ms. La'dee, our assistant teacher for the day," Noodles says.

"Hello, Ms. La'dee," the children say in unison. La'dee waves hello to the children then walks over to Noodles.

"Put your purse in the bottom desk drawer next to mines." La'dee goes to the desk and opens the bottom drawer. She sees a purse that looked identical to hers. She put it inside and closed it back up. She walks back over to Noodles.

"Now what?"

"Now we make snacks for the children," she tells her, then hands her a box of graham crackers.

******

King Nut paced the floor in his living room. He was wondering what was taking La'dee so long and why wasn't she answering her phone. He didn't want her going by herself, but Pay Pay and Noodles insisted on it being that way. He hoped nothing went wrong. Before his mind could wander any further, La'dee came walking through the front door with a smile on her face.

"Oh me God, Nut. Me had so much fun, mon. Those

little kids are–"

"Fun? You supposed to get me dope, not have fun. Me here pacing the floor, wondering if you're okay and you're out having fun?"

"Nut, I was -"

He cuts her off again. "Fuck what you talking 'bout. Where's me dope?" La'dee shakes her head and rolls her eyes at him as she hands the bag to him. She walks away and gets on the phone with Noodles.

King Nut quickly pulled out the six bricks and split one open. He tasted it to make sure it was the same shit he had tasted in rehab. The quick numbing of his gums told him it was. "YES!! Me back in business, mon," he says holding his hands up in victory.

******

Big Folks, a big Tookie Williams looking nigga, stood outside the Tower Apartments in Chicago with his shirt off and hat banged to the right. He was shooting dice with six of his fellow gangstas. "Uh, Folger's. Deuce, deuce, bitch. Twenty say I six before I eight," he says as he rolls the dice, and they slap against the apartment building wall.

"I'll take that bet," Domino tells him, throwing a twenty on the ground. Big Folks shakes the dice in his hand then lets them fly out his hand. They roll on the ground and smack against the wall. One dice land on a three and the other one lands on a one. Big Folks hits his point.

"That's what the fuck I'm talking about, fool," he says, collecting his money. His phone rings.

"What it do?" he answers.

"Big Folks, it's bad news brah." "What's the juice?"

"It's yo brother."

"Quit stalling me. What's going on with Big Country?"

"Somebody smoked him last night outside the club."

"WHAT? Nah, fam. I know you ain't telling me somebody killed my lil brother? Where's Popeye?"

"Some niggas came to the door, smoked him, and everybody in there."

"The next mothafuckin words out yo mouth better be telling me who did it."

"I don't know."

"Then you know it's finna be some smoke in yo city. I'm going to tear that bitch up until I get the mothafucka responsible for this." Big Folks disconnects the call then throws the phone against the wall. The phone shatters to pieces. "Everybody load the fuck up!"

******

King Nut stands in the kitchen watching as K-Roc cooks up the first batch of the new work. K-Roc stirs the Pyrex with the shake of the wrist and a smile grows on his face. "Look at all the oil mon! The mon put no foot on it. It's straight drop!"

"I know. Now rock that shit up and let's get it on the streets. We got money to get."

Chapter 5

Her thick and juicy ass swayed from side to side in her tight fitted St. Laurent jeans. While her hot pink St. Laurent's shirt made a good display of her big titties. Her St. Laurent heels clicked on the tile floor as Noodles enters the rehab center with five-month-old baby Dayla in her arms as she and Dayla make their weekly visit to Pay Pay. She walked into the half-full visiting area and over to where Pay Pay sat.

"There go my two favorite women in the world," Pay Pay says as he gives Noodles a hug and a kiss, then takes Dayla out of her hands. Noodles takes a seat at the table.

"Everything went good with that exchange?" he says while discreetly removing the two zips of coke from her pamper.

"Yup," she says dully before folding her arms across her chest.

"You don't sound too enthusiastic about it. What's up, Mami?"

"I've been trying to figure out the same thing, so you tell me."

"What is you talking about?"

"I'm talking about how hard we worked to get into the Black Order and how easily you about to throw it away by breaking the rules. Billy Gunz told us when he found out about us hustling out of Magic City that it was forbidden for anybody to sell weight of his work in Atlanta."

"I know what Billy Gunz said."

"Then why are we pushing weight to this nigga?"

"Baby, you and I both know how good we can eat out here in the ATL. I can't keep checking into rehab to make the chunks of money we need when we could flip our work a lot faster by pushing weight."

"Yeah, I know we're at the lowest level of the Order right now, but even so, we're still doing better than most. Billy Gunz bought our house for us, gave us ten kilos to start with, and bought us a bakery as our own little front business. Baby, we can't just shit on somebody who showed love like that. Look, if this is about growth, we'll get there once we move up in ranks. But don't make the same mistakes as Baby Red did by making dumb decisions. Now tell me what's really going on?"

"Damn, you said all that in one breath?" he joked with her as he buttons back up Dayla's clothes.

"Does it look like I'm in a laughing mood right now? Answer the question, Pay Pay." He picks Dayla back up, gives her a kiss, and starts bouncing her on the table. She laughs a high pitch laugh and he smiles back at her.

"Don't trip. I got this. I'm not going to let us get kicked out of the Order or let anything happen to us. Trust me." She folds her arms across her chest and narrows her eyes.

"You want me to trust you?"

"What you saying, you don't trust me?" She unfolds her arms and moves in closer to him.

"Of course, I trust you. It's not being in the know that I don't trust. I told you when we got married, I would follow you to death or jail and heaven or hell. But I'll be damn if I follow you anywhere blindly. We are partners and all we got, Pay Pay. So, tell me what the fuck is going on?" Pay Pay picks up Dayla and stands up.

"You know what? You're right. I'm bogus for keeping you in the dark. You want me to shed some light on things, then let's take a walk." He holds his hand out to her and she takes it. They take a walk outside and he breaks everything down for her.

******

The song, "Beauty Of Life", by Reggae Roast and Tippa Irie blast inside of King Nut's new Porsche truck as he made his way to Auburn Street. It's been a couple of weeks since he got the first batch of work from Pay Pay and he was already down to his last two keys. The streets were going mad for the new work. Not only because it was good shit, but because everybody was afraid that once it was gone there wouldn't be any more good work left in the city. So, they were trying to buy as much as their pockets could afford. With the help of the bullshit work they had left, K-Roc stretched the six kilos into nine and it was still potent. The customers were beating down the spot's doors for the shit. He even took over Big Country's and Popeye's customers. No doubt King Nut and his team were grinding good.

He gets to Auburn Street and pulls in front of a huge Catholic church, then runs inside. Following the orders Pay Pay gave him, he put the re-up money under the seat in the confession booth and left back out. He then headed back to the crib to await further instruction.

He couldn't help but think how cautious Pay Pay moved. It made him think Pay Pay was a scary-ass nigga. King Nut always thought, *no nuts, no glory.* You had to have balls to make it in the dope game. All that scary shit would keep a nigga broke, was King Nut's philosophy.

He sat on the couch watching a soccer game on TV as he waited to hear back from Pay Pay. La'dee walks into the front room wheeling a travel bag and looking sexy as hell in her super short, mint green, Gucci dress with the back out. "Where the hell you think you going dressed like that?" King Nut asks, looking at her up and down.

"I'm going to meet up with Noodles to go get your

work."

"Dressed like that? Where are you meeting her at?"

"She told me what to wear, but not where I'm going. All she said was to bring this suitcase, a taxi will be here to pick me up and to come alone." King Nut's face was filled with anger and disgust. A horn blows outside. "That's the taxi now."

"I don't like this shit," he says, tossing the TV remote on the coffee table.

"Nut, if you don't want me doing this, then say so and I won't. But you know that if you don't do things their way, they won't do business with us. Now, do you want this work or not?" King Nut waved her off and La'dee left out the door.

Maybe he was feeling a little jealous or whatever he thought. But he didn't see what need it was for Pay Pay and Noodles to have his woman to dress like a whore to go get his dope. Thinking of the possibilities of what La'dee could be doing pissed him off. He rolls a laced blunt to ease his mind before he did something stupid. Like follow her and end up fucking up their connect.

The taxi driver didn't say a word when La'dee got in. He just put her empty luggage bag in the trunk and drove off. Curious to where she might be heading, she questions the driver. "Driver, you know where we are going?"

"Yup," the driver answers her, looking at her through his rearview mirror.

"Where?"

"I was told not to say. I was also told to make sure you don't use your phone during the ride."

"You know this could be considered kidnapping, right?"

"I don't think so, lady. You got in this cab of your own free will. The person that hired me told me that this was a surprise and not to spoil it by telling you where we were going. Furthermore, I was also told if you had a problem with that to take yo ass back home. Now, does that still sound like kidnapping to you?" Defeated by his answer, La'dee exhales a heavy breath of frustration. She sits back in her seat, crosses her legs, folds her arms, and stares out the window. "I didn't think so," the cab driver said, putting a toothpick in his mouth.

After an hour and a half, the cab takes the next exit off the highway. A sign La'dee has seen before; they took the exit letting her know they were now in Columbus, Georgia. The cab traveled a while through the city before pulling into the parking lot of Sugar Babies Gentlemen's Club.

The stars now lit up the sky. She stepped out of the car dialing Noodles' number. As soon as she closed the cab's door, it pulled off. "Hey, my bag!" she yelled after the cab, but it kept going.

"Don't worry about the bag," Noodles says, walking up to her in a tight-fitting red and gold Versace dress. La'dee was amazed at how beautiful she was. La'dee cancels the call she was making to her and puts her phone back in her purse. "Come on, let's go inside."

Inside the club, a big-breasted, petite, blonde slid down the pole entertaining a group of men in front of the stage. Other dancers chilled with customers or walked around the club in search of their next dollar. The club wasn't at full capacity, but it was a nice size crowd. "Why are we meeting here to do business?" La'dee asks as they take a seat at a table near the stage.

"So, we can have a little fun."

"At a club with female strippers? I'm not into women."

"You're not into other men either, are you? I mean, I'm sure your husband would lose his mind if I were to take you to a male strip club. Am I right?" La'dee sees her point.

"That makes sense."

"Besides, I want to get to know you more." "And why is that?"

"Because my husband and I are putting a hell of a lot on the line to do business with you and yours. So, I want to at least get to know who we are putting our lives and livelihood in jeopardy for. You get where I'm coming from?"

"I get you. That's fair enough." A waitress in a short and sexy miniskirt and halter top came over to take their order. Minutes later, she returned with two long island ice teas.

They laughed as they told each other stories from their past. After a few drinks and a bunch of small talk and questions asked and answered about each other La'dee seemed to loosen up more. "Oh my God Noodles, you are crazy. I must admit, I never thought when I first met you in that church and you were dressed like you were that you would be as much fun as you are. I can really see us kicking it and hanging out more often."

"That's cool. The only problem with that is, I only hang around people I can trust."

"You can trust me." "Prove it."

"How am I supposed to do that?" "You really want to know?"

"Yes." Noodles scans the club until she finds the dancer she was looking for.

"Barbie! Come here!" she calls the dancer over. The sexy thick mixed-breed woman comes over.

"Wassup, Noodles?"

"Let baby girl here borrow an outfit and let her do a number on the stage."

"What? I'm not taking my clothes off on stage in front of all these people," La'dee protests.

"Then I guess we won't be kicking it. I do dirt like worms. So, if I ain't got dirt on you, I can't trust you. You want to prove to me that I can trust you, then get dat ass on stage. If not, then Barbie tells Phoenix that I'll take the bill." Seeing no way around it, La'dee gives in.

"No need. I'll do it."

"Come with me then. We'll go to the back and get you all fixed up," Barbie tells her. La'dee slams her long island iced tea, then follows Barbie to the dressing room.

Noodles pulls a Blow Pop sucker out of her purse and stirs it in her drink before putting it in her mouth. Moments later, La'dee comes out dressed in a sexy police officer costume. "Gentlemen put your hands together and your dollars in the air for our next performer. Coming to the stage is a very special guest, the sexy and lovely, Ms. La'dee!" The DJ announces as La'dee takes the stage. Whistles were given from the crowd that began to form in front of the stage. Noodles could see the nervousness in her face. But as Ty Dolla $ign's song, "Drop that Kitty", began to play, then all the shyness shit went out the window and she got loose. She wined her ass against the pole as she seductively caressed herself. She climbed to the top of the pole and slid down with her legs spread open. Once she was on the floor, she made her ass jiggle while in the splits position. The crowd erupts into cheers. She stripped down to her thong exposing her juicy caramel ass cheeks and big, beautiful breast along with gumdrop-like nipples. Noodles pull out a hundred-dollar bill and holds it out to her. La'dee's beautiful green eyes stared at Noodles as she crawled over to her. She pulls open the sideband of her thong for Noodles to put the money in, but Noodles rejects that offer. Instead, she slowly rubbed the bill down La'dee's neck, breast, and stomach before putting it in her thong and slipping a finger inside her pussy.

La'dee gasps and Noodles takes her finger out to taste it. Noodles smiles as she put her Blow Pop back in her mouth, leaving La'dee stunned for a few seconds. She jumped back into reality and finished her set.

After giving a few lap dances that Noodles talked her into doing, she changed back into her clothes and headed back to the table a few hundred dollars richer. "Now do you trust me?"

"A little," Noodles says, shrugging her shoulders.

"Only a little? Do you know Nut would kill me if he knew what I've just done? I mean that mon would literally kill me, Noodles. And that doesn't make you trust me a lot more than just a little?"

"Nope. Because the question that comes to my mind is, why were you willing to put yourself in such jeopardy just to kick it close to me?"

"Because you're cool, fun, and most of all, you're cunning. I feel like it's a lot I could learn from you."

"Is that right? The Queen of Atlanta wants me to take her under my wing. What is it that you're trying to learn?"

"Everything it is you're willing to teach me." Noodles eyes her a moment as she thinks about it.

"Okay, let's get something straight though. If I take you under my wing, then you can't tell anyone anything you see or hear about when you're with me. Not even Nut. Understood?"

"Understood." Noodles raises her glass.

"Then here's to a new friendship." They toast glasses. Noodles looks at her suspiciously as they both take sips from their glasses. She knew La'dee was up to something, she just couldn't quite put her finger on it yet. But she was damn sho' going to find out just what it was.

Chapter 6

His heavy fist slammed into Key's face over and over, splattering blood with every blow. "Boy, I'm gonna beat yo ass to death if you don't tell me who killed Big Country." Keys was one of Big Country's homeboys who sold weed out of a barbershop he owned.

"I swear, Big Folks, I don't know."

"Yo ass betta know something soon or they gonna be burying you next." Big Folks cocks back his fist.

"Okay, okay. Look, I don't know shit my nigga. But word is this hype named Tit Ball knows who smoked Popeye and the rest of them niggas in the spot," Keys says, stopping Big Folks from throwing another punch.

"Keep talking."

"Word is he was there when the shit went down. I'm sure whoever smoked Popeye and em did in Big Country. So, if you talk to Tit Ball, you should have all your answers." Big Folks slams Keys into the wall on the side of the barbershop, knocking the wind out of him.

"Then you take us to that mothafuckin nigga, Tit Ball, right now!"

"Aight." Big Folks let's go of him. Keys spits out a small glob of blood onto the concrete. He walks over to Big Folks' Excursion truck and climbs in the backseat. Big Folks and his crew get in, and they pull off.

"Where we going, Keys?"

"Edgewood. He and his dope fiend buddies hang out at the apartment complexes out there," he says while using the bottom half of his shirt to stop his nose from bleeding.

"For your sake, you'd betta hope we find this nigga or yo ass is grass," Big Folks says while mugging him in the rearview mirror. Big Folks was holding any nigga alive who was supposed to be Big Country's homeboy responsible for knowing who killed him. Big Country was known by all but only kicked it with a few. Keys was the only one out of those few left alive. But if he doesn't find Tit Ball and Big Folks don't get the answers that he needs, then Key's body would be the next one the coroner would be zipping up.

They drove through the apartment complex slowly. Key's head was on a swivel, looking in every direction with his stomach in knots hoping to spot Tit Ball. He sees a familiar face. "Big Folks stop the truck once." When the car stopped Keys rolled down the window. "Aye Re Re!" The woman stopped and looked at Keys." "Aye come here!" He waved her over. Re Re did a skank walk over to the truck.

"What you want Keys? If you called me over here thinking you going to run that same weak-ass game on me to get some pussy, you'd betta think again. What type of nigga buys a bitch some McDonalds and smokes a blunt with her thinking that's going make her open her legs? Nigga, I ain't no fast-food prostitute," she says, leaning against the truck and playing with her nails.

"Every nigga, bitch. But fuck all that, where's Tit Ball at?"

"I just saw him heading over to Moan's house to try and beg for a hit of dope. Damn! What happened to yo face?" she asked, finally looking up at him.

"The same thing happened to yours, bitch," he said, rolling up the window. Re Re started cussing him out as they pulled off. "Make a right up here and pull up at those apartments over there on the end."

They pull up in front of the apartments and Key's stomach eased when he saw Tit Ball standing on Moan's porch.

"Tit Ball, Moan said take yo ass on. He ain't giving you shit today," the woman holding open the screen door said.

"You tell Moan that I said he can have my money, my house, and my car. Just for one hit of that dope, he could have it all, girl," he says, dancing and singing Jodeci's song, "Feenin."

"Tit Ball, leave me alone and take yo ass home."

"I-just-can't-leave you alone. You got me feenin'," he sings as he takes his shirt off.

"Oh, hell naw," the woman says, slamming the screen door close.

"Where are you going, girl? Come back. I was just getting started. Damn," Tit Ball says, bending down to pick his shirt up off the ground. When he stood up, he was staring into Big Folks' chest. "Well damn, you gigantic negro. Can I help you?"

"Yeah, you can help me by getting yo ass in this truck and answering a few of my questions."

"Look, my mama told me ever since I was a kid not to talk to strangers and damn sho don't get in the car with them. Unless they got some money for me." Big Folks pulls out a ball of dope and holds it up in front of Tit Ball's face.

"You give me the answers I need, and this here is yours."

"Well shit, let's go for that ride." Tit Ball picks up his can of 211 beer and follows Big Folks to the truck.

As they made their way to Williams Holmes Borders Apartments, Tit Ball told Big Folks everything he heard and saw the night King Nut and his crew ran into Popeye's spot and killed everybody. "I'm telling you, mane, them Jamaican niggas ran into that bitch like some straight killas. I'm talking 'bout the shit was like a scene straight out of a movie," Tit Ball says, then drains the rest of the beer in his 211 can and tosses it out the window.

"And you are sure this nigga, K-Roc, and King Nut be at them apartments?" Tit Ball leans in closer to the front seat to talk to Big Folks.

"Big Folks, I'm telling you that's where their main spot is. I know for a fact K-Roc is there the majority of the time. King Nut comes through randomly, but they keep a squad of young ass, trigger happy, lil niggas around. They feel most people won't have the heart to shoot a kid that young."

"I don't give a fuck how young they is," Big Folks says. "You damn right. If they old enough to shoot, they old enough to get shot," Domino adds from the passenger's seat. "How many of them be in there?"

"I don't know because he doesn't really allow anybody in the house. It's always two niggas on the front porch strapped up serving the work." They pull over a block away from the apartments. Big Folks hands Tit Ball five twenty-dollar bills.

"I want you to take this and buy some work. See if you can hit their hand to let you come in and take a blast. If you're able to get in, I want you to peep out the scene. I want to know how many mothafuckas are in there and what they packing. Once you come back, I got another ball waiting on you on top of the one I already promised you."

"Yeah, now dats what I'm talking 'bout, baby. You a real playa, Big Folks," Tit Ball says, smiling, showing what little teeth he had left.

"You'd betta come back, and you bet not try no bullshit." "No worries, baby. Tit Ball is a man of his word." He holds one hand up and another over his heart. "I got you," he says, getting out of the truck then walks down the street to the apartments.

******

A different taxi driver drops La'dee off at home. She gets

out of the car and heads to the front door of the house. "Miss, your bag," the driver tells her while going to the trunk.

"My bag?" She looked at him with a look of confusion as he removed her bag from the trunk. She thought the last driver had taken off with it. She grabbed the bag and felt the weight; she knew it was no longer empty. When Noodles said she'll have the work by the time she got home, she thought someone was going to drop it off to her. She wasn't aware the dope was riding with her the whole time.

The taxi pulled off as she entered the house. The house was dark. As she walked towards the hall that leads to the bedroom, the lamp in the front room turned on. Startled, she quickly looked over in that direction and saw Nut sitting on the sofa chair. "You want to tell me why me wife hasn't been answering her phone all night and then comes stumbling into the house at 3:43 in the morning?" he says calmly while checking the time on his watch and sparking up a blunt.

"Bae, Noodles had me take a cab out to Columbus to meet her. She made me chill for a little while and have drinks with her. And you know her rules about phones when I'm with her." King Nut stands up and slowly walks over to her. As calm as he tries to make himself seem, La'dee could tell by the way his accent kept creeping in that he was so mad he could spit fire.

"Chilling with Noodles or some other mon?" "What?"

"You heard what the fuck I said! Who were you with La'dee?"

"I already told you who I was with, Nut. I was chilling with Noodles, trying to get close to her."

"Trying to get close to her for what?" His eyes furrow as he feels his temper starting to boil.

"Calm down, my love, and hear me out. If I can get in good with Noodles, I can get all the dirt I can on her."

"Dirt on her for what?" "For leverage, baby."

"Why do we need leverage, La'dee? Business is going good the way it is."

"Yeah, but who's to say for how long. You say yourself that Pay Pay seems scary. What if he gets too scared to do business with us anymore? We will be back where we started. If we can get fronted more keys of dope on top of what we buy, that would give him a reason to stay in business with us."

"How you figure that? And what makes you think getting in good with Noodles will do that?"

"Because as long as we got kilos of his drugs, he's not going to try to stop feeding us. Especially knowing it's a chance his scary ass would have to spill blood to get it back. He would have to first lessen the number of keys slowly that he fronts us before he cuts us off all the way. That way he can recoup as much of his money back as he could. Meanwhile, we stack as much money as possible. We keep cutting the keys into as many more keys as possible without losing too much of its potency. After that, if it ain't any more good dope around, we can switch over to the heroin game and rule the city with that. And as far as me knowing, getting close to Noodles would do the trick. It is as simple as knowing, to have the wife's ear is to have the husband's heart. As long as we got the strings, we can make the puppet do whatever we want."

"Blackmail her, I like that. But what makes you think she has something that big to hide from Pay Pay?" La'dee walks closer to him and wraps her arms around his neck.

"Like she told me today, she does dirt like worms. And she said if I was to hang with her, I have to keep what she does a secret," she said before kissing him.

"I think you just might be onto something. Is that the

dope?" he says, looking down at the luggage bag.

"Don't know what else it could be." He takes the luggage from her, then kneels down and opens it up. He removed some bullshit clothes that laid on top and underneath were fifteen keys of coke.

"It's all there I see," he says, standing back up. "Good, now can we go to bed? I am tired."

"Go on to bed. I'll be in there in a minute. I got to put this work away."

"Okay, but don't be too long. You know I can't sleep without you next to me." She gives him a kiss and walks off to the bedroom. He stood there a moment thinking of how devious her mind works sometimes. He wondered what more she was up to.

King Dream

Chapter 7

Tit Ball walks down the steps that lead to apartment number six. Two niggas sat on crates on the porch playing dominos. "Pig what up mane. Ouch! What the fuck?" Tit Ball feels something biting him. He looks down and sees he stepped into some red dirt and a fire ant had crawled onto his sandals and attacked his sockless feet. He took off his sandals and got them all off him then put them back on. "Damn, y'all niggas even got the ants guarding the spot."

"What you need, Tit Ball?" the chubby one said. Tit Ball pulled out sixty dollars. "Look, let me get eight for the sixty."

"You'd betta get the fuck out of here with that. I'll give yo ass seven for the sixty."

"Mane, as much as I be spending with y'all? You know what? Fuck it. Come on." Pig reaches up and grabs seven dime bags out the roof of the porch. He and Tit Ball make the exchange. "Tell K-Roc to let me holla at him right quick before I go."

"K-Roc ain't here."

"Damn! Listen, I need somewhere to take a quick blast before I get back on my hustle."

"You'd betta take yo ass in an alley or somewhere." "Hell nah, I'm too paranoid for that shit. I keep thinking the police coming every time I try to take a hit. I can't get high like that. Come on Piggy baby, let me use yo bathroom to make it do what it do."

"You done lost yo rabbit ass mind. You ain't coming in there."

"Don't do me like that now. Look, I'll give you forty dollars to let me go in for five minutes to get myself right." He pulls two twenties out of his pocket.

"No!" The other man gets up and snatches the money out of Tit Ball's hand.

"Come on. You got five minutes."

"Good looking, Louie. I always knew you was a playa," Tit Ball said walking into the house. Pig grabs Louie by the arm.

"What the fuck is you doing? You know Nut and K-Roc would snap the fuck out knowing we let somebody inside the spot."

"They won't know. We'll have his ass out of here in five minutes. In the meantime, enjoy being twenty dollars richer." He hands Pig one of the twenty-dollar bills. He leans inside the doorway and tells lil Yogi to take him to the bathroom to smoke. Louie then tells the other niggas to keep an eye on Tit Ball.

Walking through the house, Tit Ball counts three niggas in the living room with guns on their laps. One of them rolled a blunt while the other two watched an episode of 50 cent's TV show, "Power".

"Oh!! You see him blow that nigga's top off," One of them jumps up saying. Another nigga stood in the kitchen chopping up some work and swatting roaches. He had two Glock 9's in the small of his waist. Tit Ball continued following Lil Yogi to the bathroom.

"Gon in there. You got five minutes exactly. And spray some air freshener when you done smoking that shit," Lil Yogi tells him.

"Cool. I got you, baby." Tit Ball sees another nigga sitting in a chair in the hall next to a door texting on his phone. He walks into the bathroom closing the door behind him. He loads his pipe and takes a blast. His eyes get big as he takes a hit. "Damn, these niggas done got ahold of some good shit this time," he says to himself while making a smacking sound as he tastes his tongue.

After quickly blowing a couple of stones, Tit Ball leaves out the apartment. "Don't make this no habit, Tit Ball," Pig says from the porch.

"Aight, good looking nephew."

He gets back to Big Folks truck and gives him a full report. "And you say neither K-Roc nor King Nut is in there?"

"Nope. Just eight niggas. Five of them are lil niggas and they all strapped. Two of them on the porch, one at the door, three in the front room, one in the kitchen, and one posted in the hallway next to a bedroom door." Big Folks hands Tit Ball the two 8-balls he promised him along with another hundred dollars.

"There's a lil something extra to keep yo mouth shut. If I find out that you gave us some bogus information, or you ran your mouth to anyone, I will hunt you down and kill you slowly. We understand each other?"

"Understood. You ain't got to worry about me. My report is good, and my lips are zipped."

"For your sake that's good to know. Gon and get up out of here. I'm sure you can find yo way home from here."

"The whole Atlanta is my home, brotha, I'm good. Appreciate doing business with cha." Tit Ball gets out of the truck and disappears into the streets.

"The niggas we looking fo ain't in there. So, what you want to do? Wait for them to get her?" Domino asks.

"Nah, call another truckload of our niggas to come meet us over here. We finna send a message to these mothafuckas, letting their asses know I'm coming for them."

"You ain't said shit but a word, my nigga. I'm on it." Domino pulls out his phone and makes that call.

Less than thirty minutes later, another Excursion truck pulls up behind Big Folks' truck. Six gangstas get out of the truck and crowd around Big Folks' truck. He gives them their orders and they all head to the apartments.

Five of them go to the backdoor of the apartments. A large bedroom window was right next to the backdoor. That bedroom was the safe room that the boy in the hallway stood guard by. One of Big Folks' homeboys, Goonie, picks up a piece of a broken brick that laid in the grass nearby. "Y'all niggas get ready." They cock back their guns and aim towards the window and door. Like a professional baseball pitcher, Goonie throws the piece of a brick through the window. The glass shattered and a huge head size hole was left in the window. Goonie lights a cocktail bomb and tosses it in starting a small fire in the room.

"What the fuck?" Tre says when he hears the sound of the bedroom window shatter. He quickly gets up and puts his phone away. He takes the key out of his drawers and unlocks the door. "Oh shit! Aye, y'all niggas come back here and help me put this fire out!" he yells to the niggas in the front room. Tre grabs the blanket off the bed and puts it over the fire and stumps it out. The five that were in the front rooms of the house rushed to the backroom to see what was going on. Before anyone of them could say anything, shots rang out, forcing them to hit the floor.

"Check me out, Pig. I got this mint condition Polaroid camera. You can give me three of them for it," Ducky says, pulling a camera out of his bag.

"Nigga don't nobody use Polaroid cameras anymore. This ain't the 90's, mothafucka."

"Then shit, I guess I should be charging more since it's an antique."

"Get yo ass off my porch, Ducky."

"Wait a minute now. Ducky got some mo shit fo ya. How about this? Five New York strip steaks for two of them thangs?" he says, holding the stakes in his hand.

"Get yo ass on Ducky. I don't want them damn steaks you stole from the supermarket," Louie, seeing the steaks steps over and cuts in.

"Fuck what he talking 'bout. I'll give you a dime for 'em, Ducky."

"Come wit' it." Just as Louie reaches for a dime sack, the shots rang out.

"What the hell?" Louie and Pig grab their guns off their hips and rush inside.

Ducky cranes his neck inside the doorway and sees they all disappeared to the backroom. "Well since y'all busy shooting each other, I'm gonna help myself," he says to himself then reaches to the roof of the porch grabbing ten sacks and leaving the bag with the meat and Polaroid camera at the door. As soon as he turned to leave, Ducky damn near pissed his pants when he saw the three men with guns walking up behind him. "I suppose I'll put these back," he tells them and tries stuffing the dope back into the roof of the porch.

"Take all that shit and get the fuck up out here," Big Folks tells him as they push past and into the apartment. Hearing that Ducky started snatching all the dope out the roof of the porch as fast as he could.

"Mane, fuck this," Lil Yogi says, getting up off the floor. He leans against the wall in the bedroom then sends a round of seven shots from his Tec out the window. The others get off the floor and join in busting shots out the window. Goonie and the others take cover against the brick wall on both sides of the window as the shots came their way. Bullets shattered what remained of the glass window. Goonie signals for one of his niggas to throw a cocktail bomb through the window opening. The man lights it and tosses it in. Then they fired several rounds into the room before taking cover.

A few of them tried to put the fire out again while the others fired shots to keep the niggas outside at bay. They were too distracted to notice Big Folks, Domino, and Boo had crept up behind them in the hallway.

BOOM! BOOM! BOOM!

Big Folks shot one of the niggas in the chin and the bullet came out the back of his head, splattering his brains all over the wall behind him. Boo caught Lil Yogi in the stomach, dropping him. Domino popped one of them in the back of the neck with a shot from his 45. The boy fell forward into the wall and slid to the floor leaving a smeared blood trail going down the wall. Pig hid behind the bed. Louie bust four shots at Big Folks. Big Folks took cover and Domino popped off two shots, hitting Louie in the cheek and forehead. He fell to the floor near the backdoor. Boo storms inside the room with two guns in hand blasting shots. Big Folks and Domino were right beside him busting and dropping everybody in the room except Pig.

Walking through the room, they see Pig hiding on the side of the bed. Boo points his gun at him. "Don't shoot! Don't shoot! I'll tell you where all the work is. Just don't kill me," Pig says, crying and begging for his life.

"Oh yeah, where dat shit at?"

"In the top drawer over there." Boo walks over to the dresser and finds a key of dope in the drawer and takes it.

"What's yo boss' phone number?" Big Folks asks him. "It's (404)555-2311, but he doesn't answer calls from numbers he don't know."

"This King Nut's number or K-Roc's?"

"K-Roc's."

"Snitch ass nigga," Lil Yogi says lying on the floor clutching his stomach.

"Shut yo lil ass up, Yogi. You can die trying to play tough if you want to, but not me. I got shit to live for."

"You sound like a bitch nigga. If I could reach my gun, I would knock yo top off myself," Lil Yogi tells Pig before coughing up a mouth full of blood.

"This lil nigga got a lot of heart. Let me get that up out yo chest."

BOOM!

Boo shoots Lil Yogi in the chest, killing him instantly. Big Folks takes Pig's phone.

"Good looking out," Boo says.

BOOM!

He squeezes the trigger, putting a hole in the side of Pig's head.

Big Folks dials K-Roc's number. He answers on the third ring.

"Pig mon, what it do?"

"Sorry, but Pig can't come to the phone right now. He's busy being dead along with everybody else in this spot."

"Who is this soon to be a dead man that I'm talking to?" "This is Big Folks. You and that bitch ass nigga, King Nut, killed my brother, Big Country. I'm coming for both of y'all niggas. And me and my G's ain't gon sleep until y'all mothafuckas are dead."

"Fuck ya brotha. You don't want to rump wit' me, boy. Me have an army. Me murda posta boys like you for fun! You hear me?"

"This ain't no social call bitch. I'm just leaving my message. Now, pass it on to King Nut." Big Folks drops the phone on the ground and smashes it to pieces with his Timberland boots. He turns to Domino. "Now that these mothafuckas got my message, it's time to take their ass to war." Boo puts in a fresh clip and cocks his gun back.

"Let's show these hoe ass Jamaican niggas how we do it in the Chi."

Chapter 8

"What! I'm on my way." King Nut ends the call and quickly gets dressed. K-Roc just gave him the news of how Big Folks and his niggas got down on the spot and the message he gave with it.

King Nut knew it was going to be some repercussions behind knocking off Big Country. He was hoping that Big Folks wouldn't find out he was the one behind the hit. But now that he does, King Nut had no choice but to go to war with him.

"What's wrong, baby?" La'dee asks.

"Big Country's brother found out who was behind his murder. He just ran in the apartments on Williams Holmes Borders and killed everyone," he tells her while he ties his shoes.

"That place gots to be swarming with police, so where you going?" she says, sitting up in bed.

"I'm going to meet up with K-Roc and some of our soldiers. This bitch boy just knocked off one of my most lucrative spots. I got to get rid of this nigga before he becomes a bigger problem than he already is. In the meantime, I want you to keep working on getting close to Noodles. This shit between me and Big Country's brother might get really messy. And I don't need Pay Pay's scary-ass clamming up on me before we can get him to front us enough work to keep him from backing out of doing business with us."

"I'm on it, baby." He puts his twin Glocks in the small of his back then gives her a kiss before leaving out."

La'dee grabs her phone when she hears King Nut's car pull out the driveway. It was 7:16 in the morning. She sends Noodles a text.

Me: U woke?

She sets the phone on the bed and reaches over to grab the other half of the blunt that was left out of the ashtray on the nightstand. As she reaches back for the lighter her phone chimed. Noodles had texted back. La'dee lit her blunt then clicked on the message.

Noodles: Hustlas don't sleep in dis game. Wassup?

La'dee takes a hit of the blunt and sucks the smoke into her lungs then holds it in a moment as she texted back.

Me: I've been thinking about something ever since I got back. I was wondering if we can talk?

She blows out the thin cloud of smoke and takes another pull. A moment later, her phone rings. She looks at the screen and sees that it's Noodles calling. She answers it.

"Hello."

"It doesn't sound like you've been to sleep yourself. I didn't get you in trouble with your husband last night, did I?" "No. He was a little worried that I was gone for so long and hadn't called. But everything is fine." "Where is he now?"

"Some shit went down, and he had to go attend to some business."

"So, in other words, he's not there and you're home alone?"

"Yeah, all by myself." "Are you in bed?" "Yes, why you ask?"

"Because I am too. I'm just laying here all alone, naked because I like to sleep in the nude. What about you? What do you got on right now?"

"Um, Noodles, I don't get down like that. I like men." Noodles laughs.

"Really? Have you ever tried getting down with another woman?"

"Of course not. I'm a straight woman."

"Well, you know spaghetti is straight too until you put it in the water. So, how can you be so sure you're straight if you have never tested the waters?"

"Because I'm- I'm-" Noodles laughs, hearing La'dee at a loss for words.

"It's okay, La'dee, for you to be curious. And I know you are. I saw it in your eyes at the club and I felt how wet you got when I stuck my finger in yo pussy. That's what's been on your mind all night and why you couldn't sleep. And that's what you wanted to talk to me about this morning, wasn't it?" La'dee was shocked at how well Noodles read her mind.

"How did you know that?"

"Let's just say I know women. Now, answer my question."

"What question?"

"What are you wearing?" La'dee thinks for a moment whether or not she should play her game. She thought why not.

"My panties and one of Nut's T-shirts." "Hmm. Take it off."

"You want me to take my clothes off?"

"Now!" Noodles tells her with much authority in her voice.

"Okay." La'dee gets up and puts her blunt out in the ashtray. She comes out of her panties and T-shirt, throwing them on the floor. She then crawls back in bed, getting under the covers, and puts the phone back to her ear.

"Okay, I took them off."

"Everything?"

"Yes, everything."

"Beautiful. Now, I want you to put your hand between

your legs and massage your clit slowly. Take your other hand and play with those gorgeous nipples of yours." Wasting no time, La'dee does as she's told. She found it to be kind of a turn on the way Noodles was bossing her around like she was.

"Okay, my hands are there."

"Now, picture me kissing you passionately on your lips. Then your neck, nipples, and working my way down between your legs, twirling circles around your clit with my tongue. Can you picture that baby?" she says, talking to her real seductively.

"Yesss." La'dee could more than picture it. With her eyes close, her hands working between her legs, and playing with her nipples, she was so deep into the fantasy already that she could damn near feel it.

"I'm opening my legs and you bury your face between them. My juices flow all down the sides of your mouth. Can you taste, La'dee? Do you want to taste it?"

"Umm, yesss! I want to taste it." La'dee lets a moan escape her mouth as she pictures everything Noodles says to her. The more Noodles talked, the wetter she got. She never felt so sexually excited before in life. She found herself breathing hard in the phone as she chased her climax. Noodles, on the other end, chased hers. Moments later, they both were screaming and moaning as they reached the finish line together.

"Now, wasn't that fun?" Noodles asks, trying to catch her breath.

"It was," La'dee admitted. La'dee too was trying to catch her breath. Noodles could almost see her smiling through the phone.

"I'm glad you liked that. You know you are a'ight, La'dee. I guess I am going to have to keep you close. Do you remember what I said the first rule is to hanging with me?"

"Keep my mouth shut about what I see and what I hear when I'm with you."

"Right. The second thing I want you to know if you're going to be kicking it close with me is that when you're with me, you are my bitch. And you do what I say do when I say do it. Is that understood?"

"I understand."

"That's what I like to hear. Get some rest and call me tonight around six so we can link up."

"Okay, talk to you then." La'dee disconnects the call and puts the phone on the nightstand. She didn't know about going as far as being Noodles' bitch and all that, but she convinced herself she had to play the role. It was all about getting close to Noodles, for the sake of King Nut's hustle and their livelihood. But as she pulls back the covers and sees the huge passion stain that she left on the sheets from their phone play, she wonders if she was doing it for more than just that.

******

King Nut passes Douglasville High School and a few blocks down the road, he hooks a right-hand turn. He gets to the next block then pulls into the parking lot of some townhomes. He goes to the end of the parking lot and parks the Porsche truck in front of one of the townhouses. He hops out of the truck and walks towards the door where he was met by a group of dread heads shooting dice. They see him and pay acknowledgement to him as they move to the side.

King Nut, not in the mood to be friendly, says nothing and keeps moving as if they didn't exist.

Walking through the front door, he is greeted by the

strong smell of dro smoke that hung in the air. He walks to
the front room where a pregnant hood rat chick and two of
her friends sat on the couch gossiping and smoking blunts.
"Wassup, Nut?" the pregnant one says to him.

"Wassup, Keisha? Where's Monsta?" Keisha was just a
bitch Monsta fucked with to use her house for a spot. He
ended up getting too much of a feel for the pussy and got her
ass pregnant.

"Everybody's in the basement waiting on you."

"Aight." The other two women smiled and made flirta-
tious faces towards King Nut that he paid no attention to. He
had more important things on his mind.

As he enters the basement, K-Roc, Monsta, and Bless sat
at a table eating steak and egg bagels from McDonald's.
King Nut takes a seat at the table and K-Roc slides a
McDonald's bag and a bottle of orange juice over to him.

"I know you're just as pissed off as me, mon. But eat up
brotha. We're gonna need all the strength we can get to go to
war with this demon, ya know."

"Do we know where this nigga, Big Folks, and his hittas
is staying?" he asks as he takes the sandwich out of the bag,
unwraps it, and then takes a bite.

"Not yet, mon. But soon we'll know where this bombaclaat is hiding out. I got some people looking into it."

"Monsta, now that the spot over there is done fo and the
three of us will be busy trying to get rid of this nigga and
boys, I decided to let you run the main operation over here."

"Straight up? Oh, hell yeah! You know that's what I've
been waiting for," Monsta tells him with excitement.

"But we gonna need to boost up business over here. I
don't want to see them niggas shooting dice out front of here
anymore. I don't need y'all drawing a bunch of unwanted
attention to us. So that also means no mo' wild ass parties

over here and all that shit. Oh, and control yo bitch. I want to keep a low profile out here."

"Okay, I hear you."

"I'm not playing, Monsta. I love you like a brother, but you fuck this up and I'll delete you like an enemy. You got that?"

"Well understood, brah. You ain't got to worry about nothing. I know how to handle business." He pauses to take a big bite of his sandwich and begins speaking with his mouth full. "I'm telling you, we're gonna make more money here than you did at them apartments over there. You'll see."

"We'll see indeed," King Nut says, staring at Monsta's smiling face a second while he second-guessed the decision he just made. He really didn't want to trust Monsta with running a major spot for him. Monsta was a real world-class fuck up. He is a flashy nigga that loved to stunt and act like he's that nigga. All the shit he did was the same shit that got dumb niggas knocked in the game. But with the spot at the apartments closed down, King Nut didn't have any choice but to use Monsta's spot if he wanted to keep his hustle alive.

"Bless, I want you to bring some soldiers over here to stay posted at all times and keep niggas around here in check."

"How many we talking?"

"I want eight of our niggas over here at all times. I want four in the house, then I want two posted in the back of the house and two posted in the front of the house, always and at all times. I don't need a repeat of what happened at the apartments. Y'all understand?" They all nod their heads in agreement. "Then let's get to work."

King Dream

Chapter 9

"Come on K-Roc, let me cook that shit up."

"Hell nah, rude boy. Nobody cooks up the work but me. Now get out the kitchen," K-Roc tells Monsta with a cigarette in his mouth while busting open a kilo of coke to cook up.

"How you going to put me out my own kitchen?"

"Like I just did." K-Roc shoos him away with his hand and Monsta leaves the kitchen. K-Roc didn't like Monsta and hated the idea of having to have him run the spot. Monsta wasn't cut like him, King Nut, and Bless. Monsta was more of the party boy kind than a hustler. He was more trick and stunna than hustler and killer. He only called himself Monsta to make himself look hard. The nigga even told fake ass gangsta stories about himself to mothafuckas so he could establish a sense of respect from them. The craziest part is that mothafuckas actually believed the nigga's tales. But K-Roc knew the truth. The nigga was a wannabe. And if shit hit the fan and guns started busting the nigga would run screaming like a bitch before he would ever bust back. He was a pure pussy.

Monsta exhaled a deep breath as he took a seat on the couch next to Keisha while K-Roc cooked up the work. "What's wrong with you?" Keisha asked him while she bagged up nickel bags of weed from a quarter ounce that sat on the coffee table.

"That nigga, K-Roc, acting like a lil bitch. The nigga don't wanna let a nigga cook up the dope or be in the kitchen while he doing it," he whispers to her.

"I thought you said King Nut put you in charge of shit?"

"He did, but he got K-Roc watching over me like I need a babysitter or something. This is supposed to be my time to shine. That nigga had his chance already at them motha-fuckin apartments he let get sprayed up and taped off." Keisha smacks her lips and raises her eyebrow.

"And what you going to do about it? I know you ain't finna let that nigga keep blocking yo shine like that." Monsta jumped to his feet.

"What you think I'm going to do? I'm going to go stand on that nigga's head and show him who's house this is." Keisha picks up the little blue ziplock nickel bags. One by one she burns the tip of them then pinches the tip with her fingers to seal them close.

"That sounds slick, but actions speak louder than words, baby."

"What, you think I'm scared of that nigga or something?"

"I don't know. Are you?"

"I ain't scared of shit and I'll prove it." Monsta marched back off into the kitchen to confront K-Roc. Keisha turns around on the couch to get a good look at the action that was about to unfold.

K-Roc was dropping some ice cubes in the water and waiting for the dope to fall to the bottom of the Pyrex. He hears Monsta walks in and throws a mean-mug his way.

"I thought I told you to get out me kitchen." "Motha-fucka, fo' one thing, this ain't yo kitchen. This my house and I can roam all through this bitch if I want to. And fo' another thing, nigga, I don't like yo attitude. You need to check that shit."

"Stand on that nigga then baby!" Monsta looked over at her and nodded his head. Feeling himself and his newly found courage, he picked up an apple out of the fruit basket on the counter and took a big bite of it. K-Roc grabs the huge chunk of dope out of the Pyrex and puts it on a napkin that sat on a nearby plate and turns to Monsta.

"You watch yo mouth when you talk to me, you posta boy. Me give no fuck about yo house. You act like it is you that's doing us a favor by us setting up shop over here. We're the ones giving the favors. We have betta places to set up shop than here." Monsta steps closer to him. "Bullshit. Nigga, you and I both know y'all ain't got nowhere else to set up shop at this quick. And y'all ain't got nobody else y'all could trust to handle business while y'all go deal with that lil problem y'all got. So the way I see it, y'all need me just as much as I need the money I make with y'all." K-Roc leans against the kitchen counter and folds his arms across his chest.

"What is it you want boy?" Now knowing he has K-Roc where he wants him, Monsta smiles to himself and proceeds with his demands.

"For now on this is how shit is finna go down. You going to give me my respect in this bitch and stop treating me like your damn subordinate. I'm the star of the show over here. You already proved you ain't got what it takes to run shit. You messed up your chances of being a boss by getting them apartment shot up over there." K-Roc stepped up to him. Monsta took a hard dry swallow and braced himself for a fight.

K-Roc could see the fear in him. He knew he could easily break Monsta in half, but he had something else in mind for him.

"So what, you think you could've done a better job over there than me?"

"I don't think, I *know* I could've." "Okay rude boy, prove it."

"How do I suppose to do that when the apartment is all boarded up over there?"

"If boards on an apartment could stop your hustle, then

it's certain that you could never be a greater hustla than me."

"Fine, I'll show you. I'm gonna go over there and show you how a real hustla gets down. It'll be a lot better than working with you."

"Then we got an understanding and nothing more needs to be said. Now leave me be." K-Roc shooed him out of the kitchen. This time Monsta was more than happy to leave. K-Roc eyeballs him hard with smiling eyes as he left. K-Roc knew Monsta would fall for that. He was too simple-minded. It was easier than leading a moth to a flame.

Now with Monsta out the way, he could focus on his hustle with no interruptions. All he had to do is grind every dollar he could out of that spot until they could move business away from Monsta's crib and into one of their own. And to do that they had to first get Big Folks off their ass.

******

Noodles pull up in front of La'dee's house in a silver convertible Lexus. She taps the horn two times and La'dee comes strolling out. "Wassup Noodles," La'dee says as she hops into the car.

"Not much." She replies while looking disgustedly at the little bungalow style house La'dee and King Nut lived in. La'dee notices the look on her face.

"Something wrong?" Noodles stares at the small brown bungalow. Then she shakes her head and pulls out of the driveway and off into traffic.

"Nah."

They get to the mall and browse through the Louis Vuitton store. "What you think about this?" La'dee says holding a pink dress to her body.

"Yeah, I can see you doing it big in that."

"Yeah, it's busting." Noodles notice La'dee taking a look at the price tag on the low. She puts the dress back on the rack.

"What's wrong? I thought you liked it." "It's nice."

"Then why you put it back?"

"Pink ain't really my color." Noodles knew she was lying. As La'dee moves over to the sales rack, Noodles grabs the pink dress and hides it in between the outfits she was buying so La'dee couldn't see.

Noodles with several bags in hand and La'dee with only two, they exit the mall. They get in the car and Noodles passes her a bag as she drops the top on her Lexus and backs out of her parking space. "What's this?"

"A gift." La'dee digs in the bag and pulls out the pink dress with the $1100 price tag.

"Why you buy this for me? I told you I didn't want it." "No, you told me you didn't like the color and we both know that was a lie. I bought it because you liked it and I wanted you to have it."

"I could've bought it myself if I really wanted it."

"No, you couldn't. Y'all couldn't afford it." Feeling offended and on the verge of snapping out on Noodles, La'dee shoots her a mean mug.

"And just how do you figure that?"

"It ain't hard to see. Come on now, the King and Queen of Atlanta are living in a shabby ass bungalow. The Queen is checking price tags and shopping off of the bargain racks."

"What you expect when you came to pick me up? For us to be living in some mansion in the hills of Georgia or something?"

"Exactly. I'm saying y'all supplying the whole Atlanta with work why ain't y'all living up to the wealth? I put two and two together and knew it could only be one reason why. Y'all broke!" La'dee leans her elbow on the windowsill and rests a hand on her forehead.

"Well, you can blame that bombaclaat, Billy Gunz, for that. We were living good before him stop supplying Nut with work. Ever since then money has been too funny to live how we used to. We had to downsize on everything until he got his hands on some decent work. All Nut could find was bullshit dope. No one in the nearby states would serve him any good dope. He even tried to send someone else to make the purchase, but you know no one would do business that big with anyone who hasn't been approved of by Billy Gunz."

"So, y'all ended up spending more money than y'all were making?"

"Yeah."

"You telling me you weren't spreading yo hustle and making sure you had some get back money?"

"I'm not a hustla. That's my man's job. I'm going to school to be a realtor."

"It's thinking like that is the reason you're broke. You can have your legit life, go to school, and all that shit. But being the wife of a dope boy, you always got to have a side hustle and money stashed away. With the life a dope boy lives, you never know what may happen. Yo man could get busted, killed, or lose all his dope or money. You got to have a backup plan to put y'all back on y'all feet. Every boss bitch knows that. I take the money Pay Pay gives me to put in the bank or the safe and I flip it to even more with my hustle."

"What's your hustle?" "You really want to know?"

"Yeah."

"Then you gotta be down for my hustle if you want to know what it is. This ain't no show and tell, baby. I don't just put my business out there like that."

"It ain't prostituting or stripping is it?"

"Hell nah. I see I gotta put yo half-square ass on game."

They pull up in front of a large fifteen-story office building downtown. "What are we doing here?"

"You wanted to see how I eat. A friend of mines own a company on the top floor. It's where I make my hustle moves." They walk through the revolving door and into the lobby. Their designer heels echo as they walk across the lobby floors.

"Good afternoon, Mrs. Robinson," the security officer behind the desk in the center of the lobby says to Noodles.

"Hey, Edward." They take the elevator to the fifteenth floor. The elevator doors open, they step out and walk down the hall passing a tax attorney's office to the left of them. A little way down the hall, they pass the Peach City Insurance Company office to the right of them. They reach an office called The Red Walton Enterprises.

Walking inside through the doors of the pristine office, they see a waiting room with top of the line furniture. The whole atmosphere had a feel of luxury, money, and success about it. Two seemingly rich white men in expensive business suits sat in the waiting room reading *Forbes* magazines and exchanging shop talk. They walked up to the receptionist's desk. The young, beautiful, blonde receptionist was just hanging up the phone when they walked up. "Hello, Mrs. Robinson."

"Hi, Jane. Could you tell Ms. Walton that I'm here?"

"Will do." Jane picks up the phone again and makes the call to her boss. "Ms. Walton, Mrs. Robinson is here to see you...Okay." She puts the phone back on its cradle. "She said come on back."

"Thank you so much. You're a lifesaver." A man in a business suit says exits the office in the back with a smile on his face. Noodles and La'dee walk inside. A beautiful Cuban mixed woman sat behind the desk in business attire. A huge smile lightens her face when the woman sees Noodles' face.

"Hey gorgeous!" the woman says, wheeling herself from behind her desk in her wheelchair. Noodles meets her halfway and they embrace each other with a hug.

"Paris, this is La'dee, a new friend of mine. La'dee, this is my friend, Paris."

"Nice to meet you." La'dee shakes her hand.

"You as well. Please have a seat. What can I do for you ladies today?"

"I want to show my homegirl here how to make some money."

"Well, what does your investment portfolio look like so far?" Paris asks La'dee. La'dee looks confused.

"Nah, Paris. I'm bringing her in on our hustle." Paris shoots Noodles a look of shock and anger.

"La'dee, could you excuse me and Noodles for a minute?"

"Sure." La'dee closes the door behind her as she left the office. Standing outside the door, curiosity got the best of her as she put her ear to the door to listen.

"Noodles, what are you doing trying to bring her in on our hustle? Are you insane? No one is supposed to know what we're doing!"

"Paris, calm down. She's cool. We make hundreds of thousands of dollars there's no reason we can't stand to bring another person in. Besides, if she invests that's even more money for all of us to make."

"Are you sure about this?"

"I'm sure. Trust me if you don't trust her."

"Fine, let her back in." La'dee moves her ear away from the door and leans against the wall when she hears Noodles coming. The door opens and Noodles invites her back in. La'dee takes a seat as they break their hustle down to her.

"La'dee, what do you know about stocks?" "Honestly, nothing."

"What we do is get inside information from different corporations and use it to manipulate the stock market."

"Is it legit?"

"Of course not. It's called insider trading. But we triple our money on all our investments."

"I've been doing this for years. I take the money Pay Pay gives me to put up, invest it, and make a killing. My girl, Paris, is so cold with this shit. We never lose a dime."

"So, you down?"

La'dee thinks for a second. Then gives her answer, "I'm down."

"Bring twenty-five thousand to me tomorrow afternoon then we can put you in the game."

King Dream

Chapter 10

The money counter machine hums as King Nut and La'dee sit in the living room counting the week's take. He feeds the bills into the machine while she wrapped money bands around each ten-thousand-dollar stack. She couldn't stop thinking about her little meeting with Paris and Noodles. She was intrigued by all the money they were making. Noodles was right about her needing to have her own hustle. After having to scale back on her lavish lifestyle to keep them afloat showed her that. She got used to the good life. And now that they're on their way back to the top, she doesn't ever want them to see the bottom again. Paris and Noodles promised her double to triple on her return on all investments. Hearing that bit of confirmation, La'dee was all in. But she knew King Nut would never go for investing so much of his money in her new side hustle. With no money of her own, she had to figure out how to come up with the twenty-five-thousand-dollar investment before tomorrow.

King Nut's phone rings. "Wassup, Bless?" he answers. "Good news. I found out where those Chicago niggas is hiding out at." "Where at?"

"The one place we should've thought to look in the first place. Big Country's house." A sly smile crept up on King Nut's face.

"Cool, get everybody together and I'll meet y'all at Monsta's spot."

"Aight. One."

"One." King Nut disconnects the call and sits the phone on the table while he continues to run the cash machine. He runs the last few stacks through the machine and then hands it over to La'dee. "What's the total?" La'dee looks at the notepad she was writing on then runs the numbers on the calculator.

"It is... $27,800.00."

"Aight, put it up in the safe. I've got to go handle some business," he says, getting up and putting his phone in his pocket and his gun in the small of his waist. He gives her a kiss and leaves out the door.

La'dee stares down at the money in deep thought. She debates whether or not she should take twenty-five thousand dollars of it to try out the new hustle. With money still being a little funny and them just starting to get back on their feet, she had her worries about taking such a gamble. If she loses the money it would be a major setback for them. A setback they couldn't afford to have.

After weighing her options, she gathers the money. She puts twenty-eight hundred in the safe and makes her way down to Paris' office with the remaining twenty-five thousand.

Dressed like a businesswoman in her pants suit, she takes a seat in the waiting room waiting for Paris to finish up with a client and call her into her office. She picks up an *Inc. Entrepreneur* magazine off the center table that had Paris on the cover of it. The cover picture Paris had her hands steepled together with piles of money lying on the desk in front of her. She flips to the page where the article on her began. The headline read: The Money Whisper...

La'dee read the article and was amazed by her credentials. She read how Paris had and still does work for some of Atlanta's elite and famous. La'dee was even more impressed by how much praise Paris was given from the elite and famous for how well she works the stock market. La'dee overhears two men in the waiting room talking to each other about how much money they made with Paris being their broker. After hearing that and reading what she read in the magazine she was more confident about taking a gamble with the money.

"Mrs. Henry," the receptionist calls. La'dee stands up. "Yes."

"Ms. Walton will see you now."

"Thank you." La'dee walks to the back to Paris' office and knocks on the door.

"Come in and close the door behind you," Paris tells her. La'dee closes the door and takes a seat. Paris takes her reading glasses off and puts down the documents she was reading. "You're here, I take it you're ready to get on the grind?" La'dee pulls the stacks of money out of her purse and sits it in front of her on the desk.

"I'm ready." Paris steeples her hands together with her elbows resting on the desk like she did on the cover of the *Inc.* magazine. She stares at the money for a moment.

"La'dee, you know if I take this money, you're locked in."

"What you mean?"

"What I mean is this ain't going to be a one-time hustle. If you're in, you're in 'til the end. You got me?" Paris says staring her dead in the eyes with a straight face.

"I'm good with that," she replies as she slides the money over to her. Paris quickly counts the money.

"In that case, I'll call you tomorrow and let you know how we did," Paris says extending her hand to La'dee. La'dee shakes her hand.

"That's it?"

"That's all."

"Alright, I'll be awaiting your call," she says before exiting the office. As soon as she was gone, Paris picks up the phone and dials Noodles.

"Wassup? Yeah, yo girl just left. She's in... Okay, I'll

see you tomorrow night. Bye." She hangs up the phone then adjusts the cushion in her wheelchair.

After being in a coma for two months, she had awakened to find her whole life had changed. On top of dealing with Baby Red's suicide and the death of her cousin Wee Wee, she learned that a bullet had done some damage to her spinal cord and she may never walk again.

After she got out of the hospital, Noodles and Pay Pay brought her down to Atlanta and helped her get on her feet.

She took some classes online then opened up her own stockbroker company. The company became a success almost overnight. She also used the company to launder money for Pay Pay and Noodles.

Her business and side hustle had been running smooth and that's the way she wanted to keep it. Bringing La'dee in made her nervous. She didn't know her and couldn't find trust in anyone that she didn't know. No new friends was her model. But as a favor for Noodles, she was willing to take a chance on her. But that chance wasn't going to come without a close eye on La'dee. Too much was at risk.

******

Monsta stands in the boarded-up apartment serving hypes out of the back-bedroom window where he took the board off. "I got dope, I got trees and whatever else you need," he says to a couple of dope heads that approach the window.

"Aye man, if it ain't the something K-Roc and Pig and em had before the shit hit the fan, I'm good. I ain't wasting my money on no bullshit."

"This is K-Roc's dope."

"Man, everybody around here hustling has been saying the same thing." Monsta pulls a rock out of his sack and passes it to the crackhead standing at the window.

"Here try that and you'll see what I got is the truth."
"That's what I'm talking 'bout. Show you right," the man
says, taking the dope. He loads his pipe while the other man
keeps a look out for him. He blazes his torch and takes a
hard pull of his pipe. He tries to hold the smoke in but
chokes. "That's it. That's that good shit, baby," he says,
passing the pipe to the other man and still choking.

"Now, how many you want?" "Give me five fat ones."

"Give me two," the other man says after taking a
blast.

Monsta pulls the bags out of his sack and serves them.
"Don't forget to tell yo friends," Monsta tells them before
they leave.

The two crackheads walk off. Tit Ball sees a familiar
truck parked on the corner. "Say Can-Man, I'm going to
catch up with you in a lil bit. I got a friend I need to holla at
real fast."

"It's funny how you always got something to do when
it's your turn to put in on the smoke session."

"Man, ain't nobody skipping out on providing the party
favors. I said I'll catch up with you in a lil bit." Can-Man
fans him off and grabs his shopping cart. Tit Ball walks
across the street to the truck parked on the corner and hops in
the backseat.

"Wassup Big Folks?"

"You got something good to tell me?"

"Just as you expected. That cat in there is working for
King Nut and K-Roc. He said so himself. And I tried the
dope and it's their work alright."

"He's the only one in there?"

"Yup." Big Folks peels off five twenties from his large
bankroll and hands it to Tit Ball.

"Good looking out." Tit Ball takes the money and puts it in his pocket.

"Thanks, playa. And if you ever need me again you know where to find me," he says before exiting the car and running off to catch up with Can-Man.

"You want to run in there and lay his ass down?" Domino asks from the passenger's seat. Big Folks sat behind the wheel rubbing his chin and staring at the apartment.

"Nah, we're going to let him lead us to them niggas."

The block was chill. A few of Big Folks men stood outside of what was Big Country's house. They were shooting the shit and smoking blunts. King Nut crouches down behind a cargo van parked five houses away. He cocks back his twin Glocks and turns to Bless who was crouched down next to him. "I don't see Big Folks nowhere in sight."

"So, what you want to do?"

"Continue with the plan. The more of them we take out, the less of a problem we have." He pulls out his cellphone and calls K-Roc. "We ready." He ends the call and puts the phone in his back pocket.

A minute later, a red Expedition crept onto the block. The gangstas standing outside didn't notice the truck until it was too late. The front and rear passenger's side windows came down and the barrels of two Draco's came out. Bullets began to riddle the house. The gangstas dash for cover, but not before the three of them fell to the ground with fatal wounds. They pull out their straps and began busting back at the truck. Meanwhile, King Nut and Bless crept towards the action.

Boo was sitting in the house cleaning his AK-47 when he heard the shots rang out. He crawls over to the window and began returning fire at the truck. The rear window bust as a bullet hit it. More bullets riddle the rear and side panels of the truck. K-Roc gets out of the driver's seat and starts busting at the gangstas surrounding the house. King Nut and Bless run up blasting, catching them off guard and dropping two more men. Bless takes cover on the side of a porch two houses down from the men. King Nut positions himself behind a blue Mazda hatchback. Boo blast a parade of shots at King Nut from the window. The man in the backseat of the Expedition gets out and lays out a line of fire at the men ducked down on the porch. One of the gangstas catches a bullet in the shoulder but returns three shots hitting the guy that just stepped out the rear of the truck in the chest and he drops to the ground. "Bless, let's get up out of her!" K-Roc lays down cover fire while King Nut and Bless made their way to the truck. They all hop in the truck and peel out with bullets pinging off the back of the truck.

King Dream

Chapter 11

La'dee cleans the house obsessively, trying to keep busy while she waited for Paris' call. It was already six o'clock in the evening and she still hasn't heard anything from her. She was trying not to worry but that was all she could do. If she lost the money, she wouldn't know how to explain that to King Nut. She had to hurry up and get that money back in the safe before he found out it was missing.

As she scrubs the fridge clean, the doorbell rings. She wasn't expecting any company and not many people knew where they lived. She thought it could be Audrey, but she grabbed her gun out of her purse anyway before answering it. "Who is it!"

"Noodles!" La'dee opens the door and sees her standing there dressed real sexy in a short red dress with her hands behind her back. La'dee felt out of place in her own doorway seeing that she only had on some jeans, a T-shirt, and a scarf wrapped around her head.

"Expecting some trouble?" Noodles says looking at the gun in La'dee's hand.

"Just being better safe than sorry. What are you doing here?" Noodles pulls a body of champagne from behind her back.

"Came to get you so we can go celebrate." "Celebrate? Celebrate what?"

"Your first successful flip in the game." La'dee's face lit up.

"The money flipped?"

"What, you doubted us? Your $25,000.00 brought in $70,000.00. Paris takes a twenty G's cut from that. Which leaves you with $50,000.00." La'dee's eyes lit up at the sound of that.

"Are you for real?"

"Yeah. Now go get dressed and let's go meet up with Paris at her office so we can pick up our money and cele-brate," Noodles says while pushing past her and walking inside.

"Alright, well come right on in," she says sarcastically. Noodles takes a seat on the couch. "You want something to drink?"

"Nah, I'm good."

"Give me a few minutes to get dressed and cleaned up. Make yourself at home and I'll be out in a minute," she says as she hurries off to the back bedroom to get an outfit. She hurries to the bathroom for a quick shower.

Noodles gets up and takes a look around the living room. She looks at La'dee's and King Nut's wedding photos that sat on the mantle of the fireplace. One photo was of them feeding each other cake at the wedding reception. Another photo was of them holding hands at the altar. And another was of them kissing at the altar. Next to the photos was a purple and white vase made of cowry shells. The vase had artificial flowers in it. Noodles picks it up and admires the African designs on the vase a moment.

"It's an African Flower Vase. I bought it when Nut and I took a trip to the Congo," La'dee says walking into the living room dressed in a short gray and green mini-skirt and matching top. Noodles turns around at the sound of her voice.

"It's beautiful," she says, spinning it around in her hand to get a 360 view of it before putting it back on the mantle. "You ready?"

"Yup."

"Then let's ride out."

POP!

The champagne cork flies in the air and the champagne fizzles out of the bottle in Paris' hand. "Aye!!" the girls say in unison at the sound of the champagne bottle opening. Paris fills up three flute glasses with the champagne.

"To our new hustle buddy, La'dee," Noodles says, raising her glass in a toast. Paris and La'dee raise their glasses and say cheers then their glasses clink in a toast. "How does it feel to flip yo first hustle?" La'dee looks down at the racks of money on the desk and smiles.

"It feels like I'm going to be doing a lot more shopping now." They all laugh. "When can we do it again?"

"Our next flip is in two days. This time all you got to put in is ten G's. You in?" Paris tells her. La'dee, with a strange look on her face, leans forward in her seat.

"Just ten G's? It doesn't sound like much on a return. What, you're not sure about this one or something?"

"Oh, I'm sure on a return on this one. I just thought you might want to put some money up or splurge a lil." La'dee slides twenty-five G's over to Paris.

"Fuck dat. I want to eat." Paris squint and looks her in the eyes with a smirk on her face.

"Okay, I'm seeing the hustla in you. I like that. That shows me you're a smart bitch. You see it ain't shit for a wife of a dope boy to spend cheese and depend on her nigga for everything. Any bitch can do that. But a real trill bitch does what it takes to have her man's back. She does that by making sure they have a plan B in case shit hits the fan. Any bitch who can't do that is worthless. The hoe may look good, but she ain't nothing more than a decoration piece. Easily replaceable. It's good to know you're a real bitch."

"That I am."

After their little celebration, Paris leaves early leaving Noodles to lock up for her. La'dee and Noodles were alone in the office with the smooth jazz playing on the computer. Noodles sat behind Paris' desk rubbing her neck. La'dee figured it was the perfect time to make her move. She walks over to her and stood behind Noodle's chair. "You look like you could use one of these," she says as she began massaging her shoulders. Noodles' eyes rolled in the back of her head.

"Oh, that does feel good."

"I'm glad I can bring you pleasure. I'm yo bitch, remember? So, whatever I can do for you, I'm always willing to do it. Just like I know you would do the same for me." She lays a trail of kisses down her neck. Noodles' eyes slowly open.

"I can't help but feel like you're buttering me up for something, La'dee." La'dee comes from behind her and straddles her lap. Her ass cheeks hang out her skirt. Noodles grips her cheeks in her hands and massages her ass.

"And...what...would...make...you...think that?" she replies, kissing her neck down to her chest in between words. Noodle's slips a finger in her pussy.

"Because your pussy ain't even wet. So, what do you want?" Noodles says as she takes her hand and lifts La'dee's face so she could look up at her. La'dee exhales a deep breath.

"Nut is afraid that Pay Pay may get scared of Billy Gunz finding out he's selling us work. He's also afraid of us being stuck without any good dope. So, to ease his worries and mines, I was hoping you could talk Pay Pay into fronting us some keys on top of what he purchases."

"For one thing, Pay Pay isn't scared of shit. He's cautious. But never scared. And for another, Nut don't want to get involved with Pay Pay fronting him work. Pay Pay takes no shorts, no losses and he demands his money be on time."

"That's fine. Nut can handle that."

"No, can *you* handle that? Because it'll be your ass on the line with me. If I talk my husband into fronting him the work, I'm doing it off your word. And if our money is not on time and not all there, then you and I, well let's say we'll have some irreconcilable differences. Understood?"

"Yeah. So, does this mean you're going to front us?" "It means I'm going to talk to my husband."

"That's good enough for me."

"Great, now get back to making me feel good." La'dee gives her a smile then slowly licks her lips and buries her face between Noodle's legs. Noodles head falls back, and she puts her hand on La'dee's head as she rides her face to a screaming orgasm.

******

Checking out of rehab, Pay Pay gets in the car with Noodles and baby Dayla. He gives Noodles a kiss. "Hey, baby."

"Hey, boo. It's good to finally have you back home." Pay Pay leans his seat all the way back and plays with Dayla who sat in her car seat.

"It's good to finally be back home. The money we made in there though made it worth the business trip. How has business been going on yo end?" he asks Noodles while grabbing Dayla's sippy cup out of her diaper bag.

"Everything's been going as planned. La'dee says Nut is ready to re-up." He gives Dayla her sippy cup.

"That's good. How much is he trying to cop?"

"He's purchasing fifteen, but wants to know if we can front him five more."

"Front him five? We barely even know that nigga. What I look like fronting him five keys? We're already taking a risk serving that fool."

"Yeah, I know. But I think you should do it." "And why would you think something like that?"

"Because it will be beneficial for us." Pay Pay pulls the lever on the side of his seat to raise it back up.

"And how is lending them five bricks beneficial to us?" "Think about it this way, they got Atlanta on lock. So, they got the clientele to off the bricks quickly. If we front them the keys, we will get rid of the dope we got faster. And the faster we get rid of the dope we got, the faster we move up in the ranks of the Order." Noodles stops the car at the red light. She looks over at Pay Pay and could almost see the wheels turning inside his head. She rubs her hand on his head. "Baby, trust me. It all fits into our plan."

"You made yo point. I'll do it, but I'm taxing him an extra ten G's on each key we front him."

"I wouldn't expect you to do business any other way." The light turns green and Noodles pulls off. She grabs her phone out of the cupholder and dials La'dee's number. She gives her Pay Pay's contingencies on fronting them the keys. After a few minutes of conversation, she disconnects the call.

"What she say?"

"She had called Nut on three-way. She told him what's up. They went back and forward a minute in their Jamaican tongue. Ultimately he agreed to our terms."

"Aight. I guess we got a wedding cake to bake. Let's go to the bakery so we can fill that order."

"Whatever you say, big daddy." Noodles hits a U-turn, jumps on the highway, and heads to their bakery.

Chapter 12

Big Folks and Domino tail Monsta to the townhouses in Douglasville. They've been watching the townhouses for the last three days. Boo told him about the shootout they had with King Nut and K-Roc. It only made Big Folks thirstier to put them niggas in their caskets.

"Say Big Folks, we been staking out this crib for three days and ain't seen not one sign of King Nut or K-Roc. How you know them niggas is even affiliated with this cat?" Big Folks stares across the parking lot at the townhouse that Monsta had gone into. He watched as hypes ran in and out of the house constantly. He also watched every face that came and went. And he watched their every move the niggas posted outside made.

"Because Tit Ball confirmed that the same work he serving is the same work King Nut and K-Roc had." He takes a sip of his Red Bull and grabs the blunt from Domino and takes a few pulls.

"So, we going off the word of a dope head? Anybody and everybody out here could have the same work as them. Man, we wasting time. We need to be out here looking for these niggas," Boo says from the backseat.

"Nah, we going off my gut feeling, and the word is them niggas had the best work in the city. When you got the best work in the city, you don't share it with niggas you don't fuck with. No nigga that ain't affiliated with them is going to have that same work. Trust me, them niggas going to show up. Just be patient, we gon get them niggas. Watch and see what I tell you." He passes Boo the blunt.

Monsta pulls into a parking space in front of the townhouse. He gets out and goes to the trunk. He pops the trunk and looks around before grabbing a kilo from out his subwoofer and tucking it in the waist of his jogging pants. "Did you just see what I saw? That key was wrapped in gold Saran wrap and I bet you that mark on it is a black pyramid with a circle around it," Domino said.

"It can't be. I thought Billy Gunz gave orders for no one to sell his weight in Georgia?" Boo said.

"He did. It seems as though somebody broke the rules. We need to check that work out to make sure. Because of it is Billy's shit, I feel sorry for the dumb mothafucka who broke the law of the Order," Big Folks says looking out the window. "Boo, since these niggas don't know who we are, I want you to gon over there and cop some powder."

"Aight." He gets out of the truck and walks across the parking lot and over to the nigga's posted up outside of Monsta's spot. "Aye mane, y'all know where the Dro at around here?"

"What you need my nig?" one of the niggas posted up asks him.

"A dub."

"Gon over there and holla at Keisha," he says, pointing to the house.

"Good looking out bro."

"Yup, yup." Boo walks over and knocks on the door.

Keisha comes to the door. "What up?"

"I need a dub of Dro." She opens the door wider so he could enter.

"Come in." Boo walks into the house. Keisha locks the door behind him. "Wait right here." She walks to the kitchen to weigh up a dub. Boo sees Monsta and two other niggas sitting at the kitchen table busting down a brick of powder. The brick had the Black Order symbol on it alright. "What you doing with that brick?" Keisha asked Monsta.

"King Nut told me to bring that here for K-Roc to cook

up. And he told me to break down a quarter of this brick into zips of powder." Boo overheard him tell her. Keisha ties the bag of weed and wobbles back over to Boo. Boo gives her the bread and takes the weed.

"Aye, let me get a ball of that over there," he says, pointing with his head at the work on the table. Keisha looks over at the table.

"What you want, hard or soft?" "Soft."

"Hold up." She wobbles back into the kitchen. She tells Monsta to put together a ball for him. Monsta looks over at Boo then puts the order together. They make the transaction and Boo leaves out of the house. As he leaves, he passes K-Roc on the sidewalk. He wanted to put the nigga to dirt right then and there, but he couldn't make any moves without Big Folks say so or he would be in violation.

He gets back to the truck and closes the door. "Man, that nigga K-Roc is right there going in the house." "We know," Domino says.

"Then what we waiting fo?"

"I want that nigga K-Roc to lead us to King Nut. You get a sample of that dope?"

"Yeah." Boo passes Big Folks the ball of powder. "I saw the brick laying on the table and it had the seal of the Black Order on it." Big Folks bust open the ball. He dipped a finger in it and tasted it, then he blew a small line.

"Is it Billy's shit?" Domino asks him. Big Folks passes the work to him then pulls out his phone. He dials a number and put the phone to his ear.

"Billy Gunz, this Big Folks."

"Wassup, Big Folks? My condolences to you for losing your brother. Big Country was a smooth brother."

"Appreciated. And you know I'm out here in Georgia right now hunting the heads that did that to him."

"I know. Only a fool would think you wouldn't retaliate on some shit like that. A man has to handle his business when it comes to such matters like that. But what's good, you having some issues out there?"

"Nah, but you are." "What you mean?"

"Somebody out here is moving your weight around." "Impossible. Niggas know not to cross me like that." "Me and my people saw one of King Nut's people with a golden brick with the Black Order seal on it." "That's got to be a fake."

"Nah bruh, I tasted it myself and it's the real deal." "Then it's only one mothafucka who could've served him that work. That mothafuckin Pay Pay." "The new nigga?"

"Yeah."

"You want me to go take care of him while I'm down here?"

"Nah, I got this one myself. I'll be flying out there this weekend to deal with him."

"Say no mo." Billy Gunz disconnects the call. Big Folks sat the phone back down. "It's finna be a lot of blood in Georgia this weekend."

Monsta's sits inside the apartments hustling. He's been making a killing since being over there. Dope fiend Otis walks up to the window. "Yo baby boy, I need you to work with me today. I only got three dollars. Hook me up this one time."

"Three dollars? Man, if you don't get yo dusty ass up out of here with that. What the fuck I'm going to do with three dollars?"

"Come on baby boy. Let me get a wake up so I can go out there and hustle up some mo dough," Otis begs at the window with the three dollars in his hand.

"Hell nah! Now get yo bum ass up out of here!" Monsta

yells at him.

"Mane, you gon do me like that? After all the money I spent with you and all the customers I brought you?"

"You'd betta bounce yo ass up out here before I move you around myself." Monsta shows him his gun. Otis steps back from the window with his hands up. "I got customers to attend to. Bring yo ass back when you got some money."

"You wrong, Monsta. But it's cool though," Otis says, walking off. He gets around the corner and pulls a card out of his pocket. The card read:

Federal Agent Cedric Mars (HIDA division)
Phone Number (405)555-1616

"Don't want to hook me up with no dope after all the money I spent with him. Then he wants to pull a gun out on me. I got something for his ass." Otis pulls out his Obama phone and calls the number.

"This is Agent Mars."

"Hello Agent Mars, this is Otis Miller." "What can I do for you Otis?"

"You remember you gave me your card after the Williams Holmes Boarders shooting. You told me if I come across any of the other dudes that were serving out of that apartment to give you a call."

"I remember. You said you wasn't no snitch and don't talk to pigs."

"Well, it's yo lucky day because I'm feeling real talkative. That is if you still paying for information."

"I'll swing by and pick you up in twenty minutes." "I'll be waiting."

The doorbell rang and King Nut goes to answer it. Two men stood at the door holding a large wedding cake. "We're with Dayla's Bakery and we have a delivery for a King Nut." King Nut steps aside for them to enter.

"Sit it on the kitchen table." They carry the huge cake in and sit it on the dining room table like they were told then left.

King Nut walks over to check out the cake. He picks up the greeting card that came with it. The card read:

It took a lot of sugar to make this one. You're sure to gain weight with this cake.

"That's a beautiful cake. Who's wedding is it?" La'dee says, walking into the dining room.

"It's our wedding. It's our marriage to Pay Pay and Noodles in this game. Now they can't back out of doing business with us. It's til death do us part." King Nut tosses the card on the table and digs into the cake with his hands. He pulls out twenty kilos and sat them on the living room table. "La'dee, clean those off and get them ready to be shipped to the safe house," he tells her before sucking some icing off his fingers.

"I don't see why you don't have them deliver it to the safe house, so we won't have to move it from here to there." She walks into the kitchen and fills a bucket up with water and grabs a towel.

"Because I don't need nobody knowing where we stash our dope and money," he says walking into the kitchen to wash his hands.

"So, you want me to take the risk of moving the dope over there to the safe house? Now I don't mind cleaning these bricks off and even helping you count up and deposit the money. But I'm not going to keep moving the dope from place to place for you. The dope game is yo thing, not mine." She storms off to the living room with the bucket and towel in her hand. King Nut dries his hands off and follows behind her. He takes a seat on the couch next to her.

"La'dee, I know this isn't your thing, but I need you, baby."

"What do you need me for on this? You got K-Roc and other men you trust that can do that for you. Why do I have to do it?"

"Because the police never look twice at you when driving around these streets. The only person I truly trust in life is you and K-Roc. K-Roc can't do it because me and him both are automatic targets for the police. Plus, the safehouse is only a couple of miles away." La'dee dips the towel in the bucket and begins cleaning off one of the keys.

"Yeah, I know the safehouse is not far. But anything could happen in between the time I leave here and traveling there. What if somebody tries to rob me?"

"You got yo gun on you."

"That don't eliminate all my fears. Why can't you follow me there or have some of yo boys follow me there?"

"Because that's a good neighborhood and I don't want to draw no attention to that house over there. And pulling up over there with niggas like me and my boys will do just that. La'dee, you'll be fine. I just need you to do it until I can find someone suitable enough to make the transfers for us. Okay?" She doesn't answer him. Instead, she rolls her eyes, shakes her head, and turns the other way. She sees King Nut ain't trying to hear nothing she says. He grabs her gently by the chin so she could face him. "Okay?"

"Yeah, whatever. I got to get these bricks cleaned up and out this house," she says, picking up another brick to clean off. King Nut gives her a kiss on the cheek and walks out of the house.

King Dream

Chapter 13

Agent Mars and Agent Greg Sanders sat in a tinted-out Dodge Magnum watching Monsta take the board off the window and climb in. "Mars, do you see this idiot? Who the hell breaks into a boarded-up apartment to sell dope? Especially when it's a sign outside the door that says, 'Do Not Enter, Under Police Investigation'."

"Yeah, this guy isn't too smart; he can't be the ringleader here."

"Probably one of their send-offs," Mars says, taking a sip of his coffee. Sanders fires up a Camel cigarette and brushes down his Magnum PI style mustache with his fingers.

"You ready to bring the dumb ass in?" Mars snaps some shots, with his camera with telescope lens of Monsta serving some hypes.

"Not yet. Let him continue collecting his pay for the day. Well, at least until our friend Otis shows up and makes his purchase with the marked bills I gave him." He focuses his telescope lens and snaps some more shots of Monsta getting a close up of the money and dope exchanging hands. Sanders adjusts his sunglasses on his face then flicks the ashes of the cigarette out the window.

"How long do we have to wait for this loser to show up?" Mars looks down at his watch.

"He'll be here in twenty minutes. What's the rush, you got a date tonight?"

"No, but you know I don't like this part of the job. I hate stakeouts."

"You like fishing, don't you?"

"What do you mean, do I like fishing? You know I go every chance I get."

"Then think of this like going fishing and waiting to

catch the big one."

"If you want me to pretend this like going fishing, then you need to get me a six-pack and another pack of Camels." Mars laughs at him.

Twenty minutes later, Otis comes walking up to the window of the apartment. "There's our guy," Mars says, pointing at Otis.

"Give me six nice ones, Monsta," Otis says, passing him three twenties.

"I see you got some money today." Monsta holds each bill up to the light making sure they are real.

"You know I be hustling. That's why you gotta start looking out fo a brother, man." Monsta puts the money in his pocket. He takes three dub sacks and one dime sack out and gives it to Otis.

"Here's a dime on me."

"Appreciate it, playa." Otis puts the rocks in the lining of his baseball cap. "I'll holla at you later." He walks off taking his hat off then straightening it back on top of his head.

"Otis just gave the signal. Let's go get the dumb ass inside," Mars says into his walkie-talkie.

"Roger that. We've got the front surrounded," the agent on the other end chirps in.

"10-4. Go ahead and attempt an abstraction from the front."

"Roger that." Mars and Sanders get out of the car and run to the back of the apartments.

"Federal Agents, come out with your hands up!" the agents in front announce while beating on the boarded-up front door. Monsta almost shitted on his self at the sound of the FEDs at the door. He tries to make his way out the back window.

The hypes lined up at the window scatter when they see

the agents rushing towards the window. When they get to the window, Monsta was halfway out of it. Mars and Sanders snatch him out the window and slam him on the ground. "Going somewhere?" Sanders asks with his knee on his back as he cuffed him.

"Suspect in custody," Mars says into his walkie-talkie. "10-4." Monsta spit grass off his lips.

"Shit! Come on man let's work something out. I can't go to jail."

"Are you soliciting a federal HIDA agent?" Mars asks.

"I ain't soliciting nobody, sir. I don't even know what a HIDA is?"

"High Intensity Drug Agency. That's what HIDA is. But you know what? I might take you up on that offer on working something out. We're gonna go down to the agency and talk about that a little more. Watch your head," Mars says, putting him in the back of the Magnum.

******

La'dee squirms as she tries to resist her orgasm. Her hands clench the hotel sheets and her head tilts back and she strains out a moan. She dives her face back into Noodles' juice box. Noodles grinds on her face and moans while she twirls circles around La'dee's clit with her tongue. La'dee begins to squirt as Noodles twirls and flicks her tongue faster and faster. Noodles slides two fingers inside of her and La'dee does the same thing to her as their tongue continued teasing each other's clits. Moments later, they were grinding each other's faces harder and faster as they raced to ecstasy. Their screams and moans echoed off the hotel room walls as they both came.

"Oh my God, that was amazing," La'dee says as she

wipes the sweat from her forehead and tries to catch her breath. Noodles sits up in bed and sparks up a blunt, putting a cloud of smoke in the air.

"Yeah, that was nice. It's been a while since I had the taste of pussy on my lips."

"Oh yeah?"

"Yeah." She blows out another cloud of smoke. "But on another subject. I'm kind of in a tight spot right now and could use your help on something."

"What you need?" Noodles takes another hit of the blunt and passes it to her. She blows the smoke out her nose before answering her.

"Paris has a couple of clients that have some very valuable information that we need about the companies they work for. This information could ensure we make some serious cash on a couple of flips."

"Okay, what do you need from me?"

"I need you to help me entertain them."

"What you mean? Take them to a club or something?"

"Nah, these guys want something a lil more interesting than that. They want us to come to their hotel room and have a few drinks. Do a little striptease for them, you and I make out together in front of them." La'dee quickly sits up in bed.

"Are you crazy? I can't do that, I'm married!"

"La'dee it's no different from what you did at the club. It's just this time you'll only be doing it in front of two men. It'll be a piece of cake." La'dee takes a hit of the blunt then passes it back to Noodles.

"Alright, I'm in. Just give them a dance and make out with you that's all, right?"

"That's all, baby," Noodles says as she gives her a shotgun. She put her lips to hers and blows the weed smoke into her mouth. La'dee swallows the smoke and blows it out her nostrils as they kiss. Noodles put the blunt roach out, then she climbs back on top of La'dee for another round of split licking.

******

King Nut sits in his office inside of his club with pimping ass Choosey. Choosey buys an ounce of powder from him and opens the bag up. "It's fucked up what happened to Big Country," Choosey says as he takes some dope out of the bag and put it on a spoon of water. Then he takes his Bic lighter and glides the flame over the bottom of the spoon. The dope melts and begins to bubble.

"Yeah, I agree," King Nut replies while looking over the club's weekly expenses on the computer.

"Word on the streets is you made that hit," Choosey tells him as he takes a syringe and fills it up with the melted down product. King Nut takes his eyes away from the computer screen and gives full attention to what Choosey was saying. "But I be telling them, clowns, out there it's no way King Nut had anything to do with that. Shit, he was one of yo top customers. You stand to gain more from him being alive than dead." He takes his belt and ties off his arm. He slaps the big vein in the fold of his left arm before inserting the needle into it. He plunges the product into his arm and sucks it back out with the needle then plunges it back into him. His eyes roll in the back of his head and a smile takes over his face. "Yeah, that's some good shit there, baby."

"I'm not worried about these gossiping ass niggas out here."

"I feel you, baby. If I were you, I wouldn't worry about their ass either. But what I would be worried about is Big Country's brother, Big Folks because he seems to buy into what these niggas out here is saying," he tells King Nut while unstrapping the belt from his arm.

"How you know that?"

"These streets be talking baby, you know that." He slips his belt back on and lines up a couple of lines of powder with a credit card. "But mostly because Big Folks himself approached me the other day when I was on the blade with my hoes. He wanted me to give you a message." King Nut gets up and walks to the front of the desk. He leans against the desk and folds his arms across his chest.

"What he say?" Choosey lifts his head up from King Nut's desk. Just finishing off the two lines, he rubs his finger across his nostrils and then sniffs real hard.

"He said to tell you that he's gon kill everything you love until he can get to you. He said to make sure I tell you that he's sure to have a ball with that pretty lil wife of yours." King Nut's face balled into a mask of rage at the sound of the threat to La'dee's life. He snatches Choosey up out of his chair and slams him on the desk.

"He's going to do what to my wife? I will kill any bombaclaat who dares touches me wife! You hear me?"

"Calm down man! I hear you! I'm just relaying the message. I don't mean you no harm, playa. So, ease up and don't shoot the messenger," Choosey says with his hands up. King Nut realizes he was right and came to his senses.

He let him go and walked over to the tinted glass window behind his desk that overlooked the inside of the whole club. Choosey sat up and straightened his suit jacket. "Look mane, I don't normally get involved with passing messages on to mothafuckas. I mean I'm a pimp, I ain't no nigga's secretary. You feel me? I only gave you the message because I fucks with you and I wanted you be on point for whatever this nigga might do," Choosey says, getting off the desk and

112

straightening his clothes. "If you want me to give him a message for you, I'll do it. A couple of his boys have been hanging out in Magic City trolling for information on yo whereabouts. I'm sure I can pass on a message to them to give to him." King Nut continued looking out the window at the people dancing on the dancefloor below.

"You got yo dope, right?"

"Yeah."

"Then take yo shit and get the fuck out." Choosey stares at him a second. He was stuck and confused at how King Nut was acting. He and King Nut have been tight for years. Choosey was the one that helped him get his business jumping by steering all the pimps and whores in the game his way to cop they dope. And all the time he's known him, he's never tripped out on him like that.

King Nut feeling his eyes on his back turns around. "You still here? Bounce!" Choosey wanted to say something, but he just shook his head and left.

King Nut locks the office door then plops down in his leather chair. He rubs his hands on his face. Shit was getting real. His main spot got shut down and he lost some soldiers, and he accepted those losses. He understood sacrifices had to be made. So, he chopped it up to the price he had to pay to get the work he needed. But threats to the home front was going too far. He had to get rid of Big Folks and his boys before they did something to La'dee or him.

He rolls up a laced blunt to ease his mind. He fires it up then leans back in his chair and takes a long pull of it. He was finally getting back to the top of his game and this beef was the last thing he needed right now. He had to put an end to it and he had to do it soon.

King Dream

Chapter 14

It wasn't the police station or the county jail the agents brought Monsta to. It was a small office rental building in an undisclosed location. Monsta sat inside a room with one handcuffed to a wall. He was tired and had fallen asleep with his head on the table. He'd been waiting in the room alone for over two hours.

Mars and Sanders walk into the room and Monsta was snoring away. Sanders slaps his hand down on the table hard startling Monsta awake. "Rise and shine sweetheart! Did you sleep well Maceo?" Monsta wipes his face and rubs his eyes to wake up.

"Man, the name's Monsta. What y'all pigs want from me? And why am I here instead of the county jail?"

"You want to go to County? Because we can make that happen." Sanders sparks a camel cigarette and sucks in the smoke.

"Nah, I'm good on that. I'm just wondering why you fags bring me here?" Monsta says while mean-mugging them.

"Ain't that some shit, Mars. He was a crying lil bitch on the way here. And now that he took a lil nap, he wakes up a tough guy." Mars said nothing. He just sat there staring at Monsta and sipping his coffee, which made Monsta nervous. "We're here because you said you want to work something out," Sanders tells him.

"Yeah, I do. Now, what you want from me?"

"Let's first estimate the damage against you. You broke into a sealed-off apartment that was labeled a crime scene. That alone is a serious felony that can put you away for quite some time. Then on top of that, you had an ounce of crack rock already bagged up in your pockets. Right along with our marked bills that prove you were selling. It's not looking good for you, Mr. Brown." Sanders shakes his head at Monsta. "But you know, we honestly don't even want you."

"Then what is it y'all want?"

"Not you. You're just a sendoff, but we'll take you in if we have to. We –"

"We want the mothafucka in charge of the whole organization. We want King Nut," Mars cuts in. Monsta smacks his lips and turns his head to the side.

"Man, my nigga, y'all got me fucked all the way up if you think I'm finna snitch. I can't snitch on nobody. It ain't in me. I'm too real for that shit." Mars jumps up and grabs him by the collar.

"You can and you will. Or I'm going to send yo punk ass to the joint for so long yo kids will have gray hairs before you ever see the light of day again! You got that? My nigga!"

"I want a lawyer!" "You ain't getting one." "I got rights!"

"Fuck yo rights!" Mars throws him back down in his chair then sits back down and sips his coffee.

"Listen, I ain't saying shit, so y'all can gon head and lock me up. Let's get this shit over with." Sanders pulls his cigarette pack out of his shirt pocket.

"Damn it," he says as he checks the pack and it's empty. "I'm going across the streets to get some smokes. I'll be back."

Monsta gets nervous when he sees Sanders get up and walk out of the room. He didn't want to be left alone in the room with Mars. Agent Mars seemed like the badge heavy type. The type that would beat a suspect into submission. Or shoot a nigga and lie and say the nigga had a gun.

Mars continued staring at him while drinking his coffee and not saying a word. Monsta turns his head towards the door so he wouldn't have to look at him. Mars was creeping him out big time.

Mars slams his hand on the table scaring the shit out of him. Monsta jumps in his seat. Mars chuckles a little. "Sitting there fronting like you all hard and shit. I knew you was a lil bitch." Mars gets up and walks over to Monsta, leans over his shoulder, and sniffs him. "I could smell it on you. I see lil wannabe thug ass niggas like you all the time." He puts his leg up on the table and removes his service revolver from his ankle holster. He empties all the bullets out but one. "I have a way of bringing the bitch out of wannabes like you." He spins the cylinder and with the flick of his wrist, he locks the cylinder back into place. He could see Monsta's Adam's apple move up and down as he swallowed hard. It was no doubt he was scared shitless. Mars could see his leg starting to tremble. "Now you going to give me all the information I need on King Nut." He pulls the hammer back and puts the gun to Monsta's head. Monsta jumps as he feels the cold steel kiss the side of his head "And every time you tell me no or don't answer my question, I'm going to squeeze this trigger."

"You can't do this. This shit is unethical. And I don't know shit."

CLICK!

Mars pulls the trigger and Monsta nearly pisses on his self. Mars pulls back the hammer again.

"You really want to keep doing this? That bullet is in here somewhere. You never know which pull of the trigger is going to find it."

Just then Sanders walks in. "Can you believe it, they don't sell Camels in this neighborhood. I had to settle for a freaking pack of Newport," he says, unpacking a cigarette out of the pack. He looks over and sees Mars with the revolver to Monsta's head. "Uh Mars, can I talk to you outside for a minute?" Mars looks over at Sanders then unlocks the pistol and removes it from Monsta's head. Mars closed the door behind him as he and Sanders stood out in the hall talking. "What the hell are you doing? We can't afford to stray too far from the books on this one. We got too much invested in this investigation and we already lost our key informant. The last thing we need is Internal Affairs on our ass fucking our case over. What we do need is that dumb ass in there to lead us to King Nut."

"Listen, that little shit for brains in there isn't trying to cooperate with us. So, I thought I'd scare his bitch ass a little."

"Well, your technique is going to fuck our case."

"You got a better idea to get him to cooperate?" Sanders slaps his hand on Mar's shoulder.

"Watch the master go to work," he says as he opens the door and walks back into the room. Mars went into the room next door to watch the action from behind the two-way mirror.

Sanders turns his chair backwards and straddles it. "Maceo, I don't think you're quite grasping the seriousness of the situation." He pulls out the pack of Newport cigarettes and unpacks one from the pack. He sparks it up and takes a puff. He coughs a little as he blows the smoke out. "Damn these things are strong. I can't see how people smoke these things."

"Those are a man's cigarettes," Monsta says, looking at the cigarette in his hand.

"Nah, Camels, and maybe even Marlboros are a man's cigarette."

"Those are Cowboy's cigarettes. Those were made just for you white mothafuckas."

"I guess that means Newport and Kools were made for you black mothafuckas."

"I guess so." "You smoke?" "Yeah."

"That explains why you look a lil stressed. You need a smoke?" Sanders says holding out the pack of Newport.

"I can go for one." Monsta goes to reach for it and Sanders snatches his hand back.

"You want a smoke and I want King Nut. Give me what I want, and I'll give you what you want. One hand washes the other."

"You think I'm going to rat for a cigarette? You gotta be out yo mind." Sanders shrugs his shoulders.

"You know my partner, Agent Mars, used to smoke these things all the time before he quit. Now he substitutes his addiction with coffee. He used to say though, when the cigarette gets smoked a third of the way down, it's the best part. I can't remember what he used to call that part of the cigarette."

"It's called the short."

"The short! Right. He said it was the part of the cigarette that made the whole thing worth smoking. He said it was the closes a smoker could ever get to that feeling or that high of their first cigarette ever smoked." He takes a pull and Monsta stares at the amber tip as it lit up with every pull Sanders took. "You know I tried to quit smoking before. It didn't work as you see. Every time I smelled a cigarette that craving for a smoke overwhelmed me. I kind of felt like a heroin addict that needed their fix every time I ate, shit, drank, or smelled one in the air. You know what I mean?"

"He can't really think he's going to get him to talk with a cigarette," Mars says to himself from the other side of the mirror as he pours another cup of coffee.

"How long has it been since you had a smoke today, Maceo?"

"I don't know. Three, maybe four hours." Sanders takes a hard drag of the square and blows the smoke in Monsta's face.

"Oh, you got to be fiending like a motherfucker right now." Sanders laughs. "I tell you what. Tell me what I want to know, and not only will I give you this whole pack of smokes, but I'll let you off on all charges. But you only have until the time I reach the short of this cigarette to cooperate or you can forget about ever tasting a cigarette or freedom again."

"You already almost halfway away from it being a short. That's not enough time to think."

"Then you better think fast." Sanders takes a long drag of the square making the cigarette even shorter. He blows the smoke into his face again.

"Man, you putting me in a tight spot. I can't give up my peoples." Sanders stares him down and takes another long pull without stopping. Monsta watches as the cigarette gets closer and closer to the short.

"Okay! Okay!" Monsta says as the cigarette was a quarter of a pull away from the short.

"Well ain't that a bitch. That shit actually worked. The bitch nigga finna snitch for a cigarette," Mars says before taking a sip of his coffee.

"Look, I can't tell you much of nothing about King Nut because he doesn't let me that close to him."

"Then you ain't no use to me. I guess we're just going to have to pin everything on you."

"Wait a minute! I can get you his right-hand man, K-Roc.

K-Roc knows his whole operation." "How do I find K-Roc?"

"King Nut had him set up shop at my baby mama's house after the apartments got shot up."

"And what you know about the apartment shooting?"

"Not much." Sanders puts a cigarette between Monsta's lips and lights it for him.

"Then tell me all you do know." With that been said, Monsta sang like a canary. He begins to tell the agents everything he knew that would point the finger at K-Roc. He didn't mind ratting him out because he never liked K-Roc in the first place.

The way Monsta was starting to see things was the FEDs wanted King Nut badly. Even though he wasn't going to give him up, he knew it would only be a matter of time before they got him. And with both King Nut and K-Roc out the way, he could be the new King of Atlanta. And that sounded like more than a good plan to him.

******

Keisha had her homegirls, Tamika and Nakia, distract the two men that stood guard at the back of the townhouse. When the four of them go off into the thick bushy area behind the row of townhomes, Keisha climbs out of the back-room window with a backpack. She then runs as fast as she could to the other end of the townhomes to an awaiting car. She gets in and slams the door shut. "You got my pregnant ass sneaking out of windows and running to the car with bricks of dope. You want to tell me what the hell is going on?" she tells Monsta while trying to catch her breath.

"They're about to raid the house and I didn't want you to get caught up in there," he says, pulling out the parking lot and passing a FedEx truck and a fleet of tinted out black Suburbans.

"What? Why didn't you let K-Roc and the rest of them know? They're still in the house. And how do you know they're about to raid the house?"

"Fuck them! I know because the FEDs told me. And they told me not to tip them off or they'll make sure you and I both go down with them."

"You snitched them out to the FEDs?"

"It was either them or us, baby. I'm not finna have you giving birth to our son in prison and have him growing up in the system. I did it for us, baby."

"You did that for us?"

"You damn right, I did! You know it ain't shit I wouldn't do fo' you and ours, shawty." A smile broke out on her face. Monsta knew how to play on her feelings. The truth of the matter was all Monsta really cared about was himself. The only reason he even called and got her out of there was because he needed the three bricks K-Roc had there. Once the FEDs get K-Roc and King Nut out the way, he was going to kick Keisha's ass to the curb. And all he would have to do then was find out who their supplier was so he could stay in the game.

Chapter 15

La'dee and Noodles get on the elevator of the hotel. When the doors close, Noodles turns to look at La'dee. She was fidgeting and biting her nails. "Why you looking so nervous?"

"Because I am. I'm not used to doing shit like this. I feel like a damn escort." Noodles rubs her hand on her back.

"Honey, an escort couldn't make the amount of money we stand to make on this in one deal. You just need to relax." Noodles digs into her purse and pulls out a bottle and empties out the last four pills in the bottle into her hand. "Here, take these." She picks out two of the pills that had a small red mark on them, handing them to her.

"What are these?" "Mollies."

"I don't fuck with nothing but weed," she says, putting the pills back into Noodles' hand.

"You know it's a lot you say you didn't do 'til you started fucking with me. I guess I'm just a bad influence on you." Noodles picks two of the pills out of her hand and swallows them. Then she takes the two that La'dee had put back into her hand and put them in her mouth. She walks up to La'dee and kisses her passionately. As she kissed her, she pushed the two pills into her mouth with her tongue and pulls away from her. "Trust me, it'll will loosen you up." La'dee hesitated at first, but then said fuck it and swallowed the pills.

The elevator dings as they reached the third floor. They exit the elevator, turn right, and proceed to walk down the hall to room 317.

"You ready?" La'dee exhales a heavy breath then nods her head yes. Noodles knocks on the door. Seconds later, a young Italian man answers the door.

"Ah! Noodles, buongiorno!" he says, giving Noodles a

hug and kiss on the cheek.

"Buongiorno, Giorgio! This is my friend, La'dee. La'dee, this is my friend Giorgio that I was telling you about. He is the president of Global Tech." Giorgio gives her a kiss as well.

"It's a pleasure to meet you."

"Nice to meet you too." Giorgio steps to the side. "Please, ladies come in." They walk inside the luxurious room and into the main area. A fat Arab man sat on the couch nursing a glass of Scotch.

"Hello, Ahmed."

"Noodles! How are you?" the fat man greets, getting up to come hug her.

"Ahmed, meet Noodles' friend, La'dee. Isn't she a thing of beauty?"

"She is surely Allah's greatest temptation to man," Ahmed replies as he bows his head to kiss her hand.

"Thank you," La'dee replies nervously.

"La'dee, Ahmed here is the president of Sahara Oil Industries." Noodles pulls out her laptop and set it on the table. "And now that we all have been introduced, how about we get down to business? Let's see those files."

"How about you entertain us first?" Ahmed says.

"You'll get your show. But not until I check those files and see it's truly what I came here for." Ahmed and Giorgio hands over their flash drives to her. Noodles plugs them in one after the other and checks the files. It was exactly what she was looking for. She puts the flash drives into her purse and begins removing her clothes. She Looks at La'dee. "A deal is a deal." At that, La'dee closes her eyes and slowly starts removing her clothes.

The pills had kicked in for La'dee and she danced seductively to the music. She danced even better than she did that night at the club. Tonight, she was looser and more sexual thanks to the Mollie laced with meth and perks that Noodles had tricked her into taking. And to top that off, Noodles fixed her a cocktail mixed with Spanish Fly. La'dee was in a whole nother world.

La'dee and Noodles tongues danced in each other's mouths. They caressed each other's bodies with their hands and lips. The sounds of moans and the exhaling of their breaths filled the soundwaves of the air as Noodles sexually dominated her and they both chased their erotic pleasures. Giorgio and Ahmed looked on with intensity and excitement.

Noodles, with her fingers dancing inside of La'dee, leans down and whispers into her ear, "Do I make you feel good?"

"Yes."

"Good enough to do anything for me." She nibbles La'dee's earlobe. La'dee moans and slowly licks her lips while grinding on her fingers.

"Yesss."

"Giorgio is holding out on us. He has another flash drive that we need. I want you to take him to the other room and get it."

"What you want me to do to get it?"

"Whatever it takes. You do that and we'll end up being worth more than our husbands on this next flip. So, do this for us, baby. Okay?" Noodles goes down on La'dee making her squirt and squirm.

"Okayyy." Noodles licks her way back to her lips and kisses her.

"Go handle that business." They both get up. La'dee grabs Giorgio by the hand. He sits his drink on the table as she leads him into the other room.

"You being in here must be my lucky day, huh?" La'dee rubs her hand down his chest.

"It could be. I hear you have another flash drive that we need." Giorgio pulls the flash drive out of his inside jacket pocket.

"Oh, you mean this?"

"I'm sure that's it." La'dee reaches for it, but Giorgio snatches his hand back.

"I would happily hand it over to you, but what's in it for me?"

"What do you want?" Giorgio scans her body seductively with his eyes then his hands.

"I've never been with a Jamaican woman before. Fulfill that fantasy and the flash drive is yours." La'dee knew that's what he truly wanted, but she hoped that she could just flirt her way out of it. She now sees that's not an option. Giorgio was a wealthy Playboy who was used to getting what he wanted. La'dee was high as hell, but her logical sense was still kicking in. She didn't want to step out on King Nut with another man, she felt fucking off with Noodles was wild enough. But for the amount of money they stand to gain from this ordeal, she willing to go against her morals. And with those options being weighed out, she gave in.

"Well, let's make each other's dreams come true," she tells him. He removes his shirt, pushes her on the bed and she climbs on top of him. She rides him into ecstasy while being completely oblivious to the blinking red light coming from a tiny surveillance camera hidden in the smoke detector.

******

Tamika and Nakia exit the thick bushy area, wiping their mouths and straightening their clothes. The two men with them come out buckling their pants. Just then, two Subur-

126

bans raced onto the back lawn where the four of them stood. Before any of them could say a word, federal agents were tackling them to the ground and putting cuffs on them. Agents hop out of the back of a Fed Ex truck and a fleet of Suburbans. They quickly apprehend the men posted out front while the other agents take battering rams to the front and back door. "Federal Agents! Everybody on the ground, now!" The agents rushed into the house with full raid gear on and M-16's drawn.

K-Roc was getting ready to leave with Audrey who was five minutes away from picking him up. He couldn't find Keisha anywhere and his first mind told him to go check the stash. He had just gone to the basement and found out three of the three and a half bricks he had stashed down there were missing when he hears the agents breach the front and back door.

"Shit!" He quickly looks around the basement for an escape route. He spots a small window he was sure he could possibly squeeze out of.

He runs over and tries to unlock the rusty latch. It didn't seem like it wanted to give way. He knew he had to hurry; it was only a matter of time before the agents made it to the basement. He takes the butt of his gun and beats the latch. He puts the gun back on his waist and gives it another try. The latch came unlocked this time and he snatched the window open. He moves the thick coat of spider webbing out of his way and sucks in a deep breath as he laid on his back and squeezed out of the small window. He makes it out the window with a few scratches. As soon as he got to his feet, one of the agents standing outside the Suburban's that held Tamika and the other three, spotted him trying to get away.

"We got a runner!" The other agents standing around look over and see K-Roc. K-Roc takes off running and cuts between the roll of townhouses. The agents gave chase. K-Roc could hear their radios chattering behind him and he knew they weren't that far behind. He runs faster, jumping over some kids' toys and a power wheel scattered over one yard he was cutting through. A couple of agents that were gaining on him get tripped up and fall gaining him a larger distance between them. He runs towards the entrance of the townhomes parking lot. He spots Audrey's Mustang getting ready to turn into the parking lot. He flags her down and rushes into the passenger's seat.

"Go, go, go!" Audrey smashes off. Before they could get to the end of the block the tires of three Suburbans could be heard peeling out the parking lot. K-Roc looks behind him and sees the Suburbans giving chase with their sirens and lights on.

"K-Roc, what the hell is going on?" Audrey bust a left at the corner and dips the car in and out of traffic.

"We got raided!"

"What? What do you mean you got raided? You just set up shop there!"

"I think that nigga, Monsta, and his bitch set me up."

"I knew them mothafuckas weren't no good. What are we going to do? I can't seem to shake these FEDs off our ass." A squad car blocks the intersection up the block. Audrey dips around it whipping the Mustang like a maniac out of *The Dukes of Hazzard.*

"I don't know. Just keep driving," K-Roc says while sparking a blunt. He felt if they were going to go to hell or jail, he'd rather go high.

One of the Suburbans catches up and rams them from behind. Both Audrey and K-Roc bodies jerk forward.

"Shit!"

"Go! Go!"

"I am!" She dips to the left riding the bumper of a small SUV in front of her. Then she cuts in between two cars to her right and slows down before turning off the main street and onto a side street. She flies down the small residential street with lights and sirens blaring behind them. She jerks the steering wheel to the left, making the car fishtail as she made a hard left-hand turn. Then she drives four more blocks before making another left then an immediate right, putting them back onto the main street. Just up ahead, two squad cars had the street blocked off. She had nowhere to turn.

She gives K-Roc a quick kiss then snatches the blunt from him and takes a hard pull of it. "Buckle up, baby!"

"Let's do this." They both buckle their seatbelts and Audrey puts the pedal to the metal. The engine roars and the exhaust hums as she heads straight for them. When they get about a car's distance away, the squad cars move out the way. When they do, Audrey and K-Roc both seen the spike strip the squad cars were hiding, but it was too late. They hit the spike strip blowing out the front driver's tire. The car fishtails a little and spins out, slinging the passenger side of the car into a telephone pole. Audrey tried to keep going but she only made it eight blocks away before the shredded rubber from the tire got caught up in the wheel well and the car refuses to go any further. They both get out and try to make a run for it, but the agents were already on them. They cuffed both of them and put them in separate cars.

Mars and Sanders pull up in their Magnum. Mars gets out and walks straight up to the car K-Roc sat in. He opens K-Roc's door. "Well, if it isn't my nigga, K-Roc."

"I don't know you and you don't know me, mon. So, don't play like we're friends, you hear?"

"I hear you K-Roc. But hear me. You and I going to have a long talk and get to know one another."

"We have nothing to talk about."

"Agent Mars! Look at what we found in the trunk!" An agent yells, holding up two kilos of dope.

"That's not ours."

"Well, it seems like we do have something to talk about after all."

Chapter 16

La'dee sat in Paris' office with her and Noodles. Paris smiles as she goes over the files on the three flash drives. "You're smiling, so I take it that's exactly what you needed?" Paris takes out one flash drive and puts in another.

"La'dee, this is exactly what we all needed." She scrolls down the list. "I'm going in heavy on this one. Noodles, you in?"

"And you know it," she replies before putting a stick of WinterFresh gum in her mouth.

"La'dee, what about you?" "How heavy we talking?"

"I say we all put in a quarter of a million apiece on this." "A quarter of a million? Woman, are you mad? I don't have a quarter of a million dollars. I only have fifty grand, which I just made from our last flip."

"You can't borrow it from your husband?"

"He doesn't have that kind of money right now he just re-upped." Paris exhales a deep breath.

"What about assets? You got any assets in your name?" "The only thing Nut has in my name is the club."

"Hold up." Paris types something in on the computer and scrolls through a search list 'til she finds what she was looking for. She clicks on her search and reads it.

"I tell you what I can do for you. I will front you the money."

"You will? Thank you. I promise you that I'll pay you back."

"Don't thank me just yet. I don't just go around loaning out so much money without protecting my own ass. If I do this, you have to bring me the fifty G's you have and allow me to put a lien on the club. That way if you try to fuck me over, the club comes to me. I just checked out what the club is worth. Property wise, it isn't worth nothing but $150,000. I'm sure you all probably have a little more invested into it, so I ain't tripping."

"How can I fuck over you when the money from the flip comes to you first?"

"Not this one. This one will be too large of a kickback to be a cash-out. They would have to send it straight to your account," Noodles tells her.

"I don't know about this. Nut would literally lose his mind if he found out I put his club on the line. That club is his baby." Noodles gets up, walks behind La'dee and begins massaging her shoulders.

"La'dee, we stand to make $1.5 million apiece on this deal if we all come in with a quarter of a million dollars. Think about what you and Nut could do with all that money. With that type of cash, you can open up your own real estate company." La'dee had told Noodles before that her dream was to open up her own high-end real estate company once she finished school. She worried about having the money to do it. With $1.5 million that could buy her first high-end house to flip. So that definitely had her attention. La'dee was smart but she was also gullible when it came to people, she fond of. Noodles knew that and played on it to the fullest.

La'dee sees both of their eyes were concentrated on her as if all their hopes of success boiled down to what she was to say next. She looks to the right of her.

"Noodles, you sure about this?"

"Sure, enough to put my last two hundred and fifty thousand in." La'dee thinks to herself a moment. "Look, have I or Paris ever steered you wrong?"

"No." Noodles stop rubbing her shoulders, kneels in front of La'dee, and looks her in the eyes.

"So, you have no reason not to trust us on this one.

Think about what you had to go through to even get the information we needed for this flip. If you ask me, you already got a lot more invested in this than some damn club. So, don't get cold feet now." Paris looks at her watch.

"I don't mean to rush you to a decision La'dee, but we have less than a couple of hours to have our investment in before the market closes. So, what's it going to be?" Noodles holds La'dee's hands in hers and gives her a pleading look she couldn't ignore.

"Okay, I'm in. But as soon as the flip pays out, the lien has to be taken off the club." Noodles kisses her hands and mouths the words Thank You to her.

"That's fine. I have a lien contract template on my computer that I can edit a little bit and print out for us. And Noodles is a licensed notary, so that'll save us any trips outside the office." Paris pulls the lean contract up on the computer. She does a little editing to it then prints out two copies. She hands them to La'dee and La'dee quickly glances over them before signing her name on both documents. Noodles pulls out her notary device and stamps the documents. She hands them to Paris. "I'll take this one and you keep this copy." She hands a copy to La'dee. "I'll see you tomorrow. And stop worrying. I got this," Paris says, stacking and shuffling the papers on her desk.

"I will try. See you tomorrow." La'dee and Noodles gets up and heads out the door. Noodles looks back at Paris and winks her eye at her before leaving.

******

"This one is going to be a hard one to crack, Mars. K-Roc's the type that'll rot away in the worst prison you could ever send before he ever rolls over on anyone, especially King Nut," Sanders says as he and Mars watch K-Roc from behind the mirror. Mars stirs his coffee with a straw as he looks on.

"I'll get him to talk." Sanders slowly turns his head towards Mars.

"By the books, Mars."

"Don't worry. It will be." Mars walks out of the viewing room into the interrogation room where K-Roc sat. He pulls out the chair on the other side of the table. He takes a seat and props his legs up on the table as he reads K-Roc's file. "Umm um," he says shaking his head. "Boy, you in a whole world of shit here, K-Roc." K-Roc sat there with his arms crossed. Mars points at the file in his hand and without looking up he continues. "With your past record and all these new charges, you'll now be facing, the courts will surely hang you. Hell, the only light of day you'll ever see again is on the prison yard. But we can work something out and have you back on the streets in about five, maybe six, years if you cooperate."

"Me don't make no deals with the police. You can go fuck yourself you posta boy. No rat boy over here. Me don't see the light of day again, oh well. Me know what me signed up for when I got in the game, you know. Me real gangsta, so yo threats of life in prison don't scare me. Me battle it out in court with me lawyers," K-Roc says, slamming his hand down on the table with a frown on his face.

Mars tosses the file on the table, takes his legs off it, and then he slowly claps his hands. "I'll give it to you, K-Roc. You're the real deal. Just as gangsta as they come and know how to hold yo tongue. But you know what? I've been in law enforcement for over eighteen years. And you know what such experience has taught me? It taught me every man has a weakness. And with the right amount of pressure and knowing where to apply it, any man's weakness could be exposed." K-Roc grunts and looks up at the ceiling. "Oh, you don't think fat meat is greasy." Mars walks over to the mirror and nods his head. Moments later, a uniformed officer opens the door. "I want you to get up and come take a lil walk with me."

"For what?"

"Well if you get yo ass up and walk with me, you'll find out." K-Roc reluctantly stood up. He towered over the 5'11" Mars by four inches. Mars cuffed his hands in front of him then led him into a mirror room across the hall.

"What are we doing in here?"

"Finding your weak spot. Now, if you don't care about saving your own ass, what about saving hers?" Mars flips a switch, and the other side of the mirror comes into view.

On the other side of the mirror, Audrey sat across the table from Agent Sanders. "Ms. Persons, all you have to do is write a statement saying that K-Roc forced you into a high-speed chase with us, the dope we found in the car was his and we'll let you go."

"Who's K-Roc? I don't know no K-Roc." "Then who was the man in the car with you?"

"There was a man in the car with me?" Sanders slammed his notepad and pen on the table and jumped up from his seat. He was getting irritated and fed up with Audrey playing dumb with him.

"You want to keep playing dumb and covering for that dirtbag boyfriend of yours, then you can do his time for him too. And while you doing time in the slammer, you can bet your pretty little ass he's going to have some other bitch by his side to replace you."

"You think she'll have a big booty? Because I always picture him with a woman with a huge ass." Audrey leans back in her seat and puts her hands behind her head and smiles up at the ceiling. "I'm going to have fun at night in my cell with my hand in my pants imaging him tearing her ass up from the back." K-Roc was laughing on the other side of the mirror. He was proud of how Audrey didn't fold under pressure. She was more real than most niggas in the game. She would do whatever for him, kill, steal, die, and even do life in prison. She was his ride or die without a doubt.

"That's good, really funny. You're quite the comedian, Ms. Persons. And I'm glad you think spending the majority of the rest of your life in prison is funny. I'm sure the judge would get a good laugh out of it too. But you know what isn't funny? You giving birth to that baby you're carrying in a small 6x9 cell." Audrey took her hands from behind her head and sat up straight. Her face became serious. K-Roc looked stunned on the other side of the mirror.

"How do you know I'm pregnant?"

"You let the paramedics know when they checked you out before we brought you in."

"I'm suing the fuck out them bitches. They broke the doctor-patient confidentiality clause. They ain't supposed to tell you that."

"Actually, they did. By law, we have to be aware of any serious medical conditions you have so we know how to better care for you. But that should be the least of your concern. You should be worried more about your child growing up without its mother. You want to be there to see the child takes its first steps, say it's first words. Hell, with the time you get from this case, you want to be able to see your child graduate from high school. It's a shame how K-Roc would let his pregnant girlfriend take the rap for him." Audrey turns her head away from Sanders and he immediately reads her body language.

"Oh, wait a minute. He doesn't know, does he? You

didn't tell him you're four months pregnant?"

"No! And it's not your business to tell him either. I'll tell him when I'm good and damn ready to."

"Why? Let me guess, you're afraid he's going to own up to all this to keep you from going to prison?"

Sander's words weren't shaking Audrey. She stood firm on taking the rap for K-Roc. But it did get to K-Roc. "Let her go. You need to make sure I'm out in five years and I'll do whateva you need me to do."

"Sounds reasonable. Let's go back in there and talk."

King Dream

Chapter 17

King Nut keeps looking out the windows and clutching his gun off every little noise he hears. With Big Folks after him and finding out through some cats out at the townhouses that Monsta's spot got raided, his paranoia was at an all-time high. He's been calling K-Roc's phone all night while La'dee calls Audrey's and hasn't got an answer. He also had La'dee check the jails and hospitals to see if either of them were there. He didn't know what to think.

"Nut, baby, you have to relax before you worry yourself to death. I'm sure K-Roc is fine. If they had him, we would've known by now. You said yourself that your homeboy by the townhouses said he saw K-Roc dip out on the police."

"You're not understanding, La'dee. It's not just that. It's also the fact we just borrowed five bricks and if K-Roc doesn't have them on him then that means over three of them just got caught up. We can't afford that loss. We haven't even got back on our feet good enough yet."

"I know, but trust it's going to work out." Before he could give her a pessimistic reply, his phone rings.

"Hello."

"Yeah mon, it's me."

"K-Roc? Where are you? I've been trying to reach you all night."

"The spot got raided." "I heard."

"I lost me phone running from the police. Monsta that posta boy and him bitch ratted us out, you know."

"What? Where's the work?"

"Them run off with it just before the FEDs kicked in the door. All three bricks and some are gone thanks to them."

"Shit!" King Nut says, slamming his fist down on the

molding around the window.

"Listen mon, me and Audrey are laid low in a telly just outside of town 'til things cool down. I suggest you do the same, you hear. I'll call and meet up with you in a couple of days so we can figure this shit out."

"Aight, one."

"One." King Nut disconnects the call then turns his attention to La'dee. "We got Big Folks and gangstas gunning for us, we owe Pay Pay and we got HIDA on our ass. Shit is bad, La'dee. We got to hit it back to Jamaica. I got to go find a way to quickly get off the rest of the bricks. I already know someone that'll take the club and both houses off our hands for a reasonable price." King Nut grabs his keys off the counter and heads for the door.

"That's where you finna go now?"

"No, Pay Pay said he needed me to meet up with him. I'm going to see what he wants to talk about. Hopefully, he doesn't know about any of this. I need to keep him cool until we get off everything and leave. The last thing we need right now is another enemy." He leaves out and she closes the door behind him. She was trying not to panic. The last thing La'dee needed was for him to try to sell the club and find out it's a lien on it. She had to check with Paris about the flip, but it was still hours before the market closed. She could only hope that King Nut stayed busy with other business until then.

The song, "Drawing Symbols", by YoungBoy Never Broke Again played through the Pioneer speakers in King Nut's Porsche truck. The urgency in Pay Pay's voice on the phone earlier made him nervous. His mind couldn't help but wonder what could be so important that he requested that he meet with him ASAP. All he knew was it couldn't be nothing good.

His phone rings as he walks through the gates of Six Flags Over Georgia. "Hello."

"I see you made it."

"I just walked through the entrance. Where are you?"

"It's a ride on the far north side of the park called the Tornado. Go there and get on it and I'll meet you there," Pay Pay says before ending the call.

King Nut quickly scanned a nearby map then made his way to the Tornado ride. He gets there and sees no sign of Pay Pay. The line for the ride was almost a quarter of a mile long and the summer heat was blazing, causing him to sweat up a storm. All of which only added more to his frustration. A vendor walked past pushing a cart of beverages for sale. King Nut waves him over and buys two ice-cold bottled waters. He twists the cap off one of them, drained the bottle in seconds, and tossed it to the side.

Almost an hour later, the line was even longer behind him than it was in front of him. However, there still was no sign of Pay Pay. He downs his last bottle of water and calls Pay Pay's phone back a few times but gets no answer. By this time, the ride had returned with its passengers exiting. The line got to moving again and it was now his turn to board. He gets in the last row on the rollercoaster and just as he buckles up, Pay Pay hops in beside him.

"You finally decided to show up?"

"I don't do lines." Pay Pay says, buckling in.

"What is it you want to talk about?" The ride operator comes by and checks their safety belts.

"Our business dealings." The ride operator pressed a button, and the rollercoaster began to move.

"What about it?"

"Your current troubles put our business dealings in jeopardy. I heard Big Folks connected Big Country's murder to you. And I hear he's in town making a mess trying to find you. That's not good" The rollercoaster rolls up the tracks.

"I ain't worried about Big Folks."

"Well, I am. Because you still owe me for five bricks and a dead man can't pay."

"I'll take care of Big Folks. And I'll have yo money in a week."

"I also hear HIDA is on yo ass. You're too hot to fuck with right now. I doubt you'll make it a week before Big Folks or HIDA gets ahold of you. So, just drop those five bricks off at the confession booth, and let's cut all ties."

"That's not going to happen. Your hands are just as dirty as mines, Pay Pay. Did you forget you were the one that told me to murk Big Country? And the word I got from the streets this morning was that Billy Gunz got in town last night and didn't seem to be in a good mood either. I'm pretty sure word got to him about someone serving me his weight out here. Seeming I'm already a dead man, as you say, then I wouldn't mind feeding Big Folks and Billy Gunz the information they need." King Nut could see Pay Pay's facial expression change. He didn't look so confident anymore. Pay Pay nervously rubs his face. If that was true, then Billy Gunz was about to fuck his whole world up. "So, it sounds like we're in this together, bruh. I ain't trying to make things hard on you or ask you for anything unreasonable. All I'm asking is for you to give me a lil time to get shit together and I'll have your money." They braced their selves as the rollercoaster reached the top then came racing down. It sped through a loop and raced around the curves then did it all over in reverse before stopping back in front of the ride's entrance.

"You have four days. If you don't have my money by then, I'll make sure you won't live long enough to tell anybody shit." The grim look on Pay Pay's face showed King Nut that he might've underestimated Pay Pay a little and that he just might have some killa in him after all.

The ride operator pressed a button, and the safety bars came up.

"Fair enough. I'll have my wife drop that paper off to you in four days," King Nut says, unbuckling his safety belt.

"You still call her your wife? You a better man than I am on that one." Pay Pay chuckles.

"Why you say that?"

"I thought she left you." King Nut gives him a look of confusion.

"Why would you think something like that?" "Never mind, it ain't none of my business." "What is it, mon? Tell me!"

"You know La'dee and Noodles been hanging out a lot lately, right?"

"So." They climb out of the rollercoaster and start walking away from the ride.

"Well, they became really close. I guess La'dee felt comfortable enough with Noodles to tell her lil secret."

"What secret?"

"That she's been having an affair with some rich Italian dude. She also said that she was about to leave you, take all your money, and start a new life with him."

"You lying!"

"What the fuck do I stand to gain by lying to you about this? I was surprised it ain't raised an eyebrow for you when she sold the club."

"She didn't sell me club."

"She sold your club to a friend of ours yesterday. She told my wife that she couldn't believe you were dumb enough to put the club in her name." King Nut was boiling mad.

"That's bullshit! Where I'm from lies like that would get a man killed and his tongue cut out. I know me La'dee would never do that to me." Pay Pay ignores him and calls Noodles' phone.

"Baby, send King Nut the video...I don't give a fuck if that's yo friend or not. Do it now!" He ends the call and a few moments later King Nut's phone goes off.

"Noodles secretly videotaped it to use it as leverage against La'dee if she ever tried to fuck her over." King Nut clicks on the message and plays the video. The video showed La'dee kissing all over Giorgio and going down on him. H watches as she got on all fours on the bed and screamed as he pounded her out from the back. King Nut was so angry, he didn't realize how hard he was squeezing the phone until it broke into pieces in his hands. His eyes begin to water.

"I'll see you and four days." He stormed off before a tear could exit the ducts of his eyes. Pay Pay pulls out his phone.

"Yeah baby, he took the bait. Now it's time to move on to the next step in the plan. Call me when it's done." He ends the call, and a smile creases his face. King Nut was playing right into his plan. He knew King Nut wouldn't last four days with all the heat he had on him. And once he was out the way, he would settle things between him and Billy Gunz. He just had to dodge him until then.

Chapter 18

Monsta and Keisha sat inside a seedy motel in East Atlanta bagging up zips of the work they stole.

"Didn't I tell you it all was going to work out, baby?"

"Yes, you did bae."

"Now that the FEDs got K-Roc, nothing is going to stop us from getting to the top."

"What about King Nut?"

"What about him? That's my boy and all, but it's only a matter of time before the FEDs catch up with him too.

"You think K-Roc's going to give him up?"

"Nah, he too solid for that. But as thirsty as the FEDs are for King Nut, they'll find some shit to stick to him. once he's out the picture, Atlanta will be all ours." A knock on the door disturbed the rhythm of their conversation. They both stare oddly at the door a moment. It was odd someone would be knocking at their room door. No one knew they were there. Monsta went straight for his Glock 40 on the nightstand. "Who is it?" he yells to the door from the side of the bed.

"Front desk."

"What do you want? We're busy."

"I'm sorry to disturb you, sir, but we just need a quick signature from you on the sign-in form. You forgot to sign it when you checked in."

"We'll sign it later."

"That's not going to work for us, sir. Since it was a debit card used, we need a signature authorizing us to charge the funds to your card. If I can't get that signature now, we're going to have to ask you to leave."

"Just a minute."

"That's a woman. I thought the person working the front

desk was a man." He turns to Keisha.

"Why you ain't use cash?"

"Cuz I spent the money you gave me shopping." Monsta smacks his lips.

"Get the door."

"You want me to get it? You got the gun."

"Bitch, get the fucking door." Keisha smacks her lips and rolls her eyes, then stomps off to the door. She opens the door and a woman stood there tapping her pen on a clipboard.

"Sign here please," she says, handing her the clipboard and pen. Keisha quickly scribbles down her signature and hands the pen and clipboard back to the woman.

"Bring us some more towels too."

"I'll have the maids get on it right away." The woman walks off and Keisha closes the door.

"You can put yo gun away now." Monsta sat the gun back on the nightstand. He gets a text message on his phone. "What's that about?" she asks as he reads the message and smiles.

"That's Bird, he wants to stop by and pick up four and a baby. I'm telling you, baby, we're going to sell out of this shit within a couple of weeks. I got to find King Nut's plug before that happens."

"And just how do you plan on doing that?"

"I don't know. But I don't care if I got to stalk his ass day and night to find out, I'm going to find out." Another knock at the door interrupts their conversation again. Monsta snatches up the gun again off the nightstand.

"What are you doing?"

"Last I check, Bird didn't have wings. It ain't no way he got here that fast."

"Who is it?"

"Housekeeping."

"Put the gun away. That's the maids with the fresh towels I asked for." Monsta puts the gun down and Keisha opens the door. As soon as the door opens, she's smashed in the face with the butt of a gun and is snatched up. Audrey puts the gun to the side of her head and closes the door behind her. Monsta quickly grabs his gun and aims it at Audrey.

"Drop yo piece or I'll drop yo bitch!"

"Kill that bitch, I don't give no fuck. You'll be doing me a favor."

"Monsta!" Keisha yells with shock on her face and fear in her voice.

"I ain't playing with yo snitch ass, Monsta. Drop yo piece."

"I ain't playing either. Kill her if you want, I ain't dropping this gun. I know if I do, you're going to kill me anyway. So, what's going to happen is, I'm finna take this work right here and split out that door." Monsta starts loading the work into a backpack while his gun stayed trained on Audrey.

"You're right, either way, you're dead. But nigga, you ain't got no room to negotiate with me. We both know yo pussy ass ain't going to pull the trigger anyway. You couldn't squash a grape in a fruit fight."

"Try me and see. I wish that bitch ass nigga of yours K-Roc was here. I would gladly put a bullet in his ass."

Keisha's eyes grew big at what she sees rising up behind Monsta. Neither of them heard him creep in through the bathroom window.

"Monsta, behind you!" Keisha screamed. Monsta didn't have enough time to react before K-Roc had a straight razor to his neck.

"Be careful what you bombaclaat wish for." And in one swift motion the blade slices across his jugular. A fountain of blood began gushing out and he fell to the floor dead. Keisha screamed from the top of her lungs.

"Bitch, shut the fuck up!"

POW! POW! POW!

Audrey puts a bullet in her head and when she dropped, she put two more in her stomach. K-Roc grabbed the backpack with the work, and they head for the door. A knock at the door stopped them in their tracks. K-Roc pulls his gun out and Audrey readies hers.

"Who it is?"

"It's Bird." She opens the door a crack. A man in a white tee and an Atlanta Braves fitted cap.

"Wassup?"

"Where that nigga, Monsta, at?" "He ain't here right now."

"He ain't here? That nigga was supposed to have a four and a split waiting on me. I know that nigga didn't have me come all the way out here for nothing." K-Roc comes to the door moving Audrey out the way.

"I got it right here for you, mon," he says, passing Bird four and a half zips.

Bird stuffs the work in his draws, hands K-Roc the money, and then leaves. K-Roc turns to Audrey. "We outta here."

******

The stock market had been closed for almost two hours now and La'dee hadn't heard anything from Paris. She tries calling her office number but gets no answer. She calls her cell phone and gets no answer on it either. She then calls Noodles' phone. Noodles answer on the fifth ring.

"Wassup?"

"Wassup is the market closed two hours ago and Paris

isn't answering her phone. I need to know what's going on with the flip before I flip out."

"Calm down, La'dee."

"I can't calm down. Nut is making plans to sell the club. If he sees the deed has a lien on it and stops him from making the sale, he's going to snap."

"Like I said, La'dee, calm down. Paris had a physical therapy appointment today. I was just going to text you and let you know we're supposed to meet her at the Hilton Hotel downtown in about an hour."

"So, the flip went well?"

"Why else would we be meeting her at the hotel? We're going there so she can transfer the funds into our accounts, and we can do a lil celebrating."

"Are you serious? We really made 1.5 million dollars?"

"Yeah, I'm serious. I don't joke about money. Listen, get your lil sexy self together and meet us at the hotel in an hour so we can get this money. Room 251. Make sure you get all dolled up for me and wear something sexy."

"I can do that for you."

"Cool, see you in an hour." Noodles ends the call.

La'dee exhales a heavy breath. With her mind now at ease, she jumps and the shower and begins getting ready.

******

After purchasing a replacement phone, King Nut goes to his club. As he pulls up, he sees construction workers coming in and out of the club doing reconstruction. He gets out his Porsche truck and rushes over to the foreman.

"What the hell you doing to my club?" The foreman removes his safety goggles and looks him up and down.

"I don't quite gather what you saying, sir. Because this here club belongs to Ms. Walton."

"I don't know no Ms. Walton and I've been the owner of this club for years."

"All I know is according to the paperwork she gave me, so I could obtain the permits, says she acquired this club yesterday from its former owner, Mrs..." He looks at the forms on his clipboard. "Mrs. La'dee Henry." He shows King Nut La'dee's signature on the form of sale.

"That's my wife! She can't sell me club! What about my property and the rest of me shit inside?" The foreman flips to another page on the clipboard.

"According to their deal, the club and everything in it now belongs to Ms. Walton. But she did pay one of my workers to pack up everything in the office and drop it off at a storage facility at Mrs. Henry's request." King Nut looked as if he was about to fall to pieces. "Sorry, my friend. I guess you and the missus have some serious business to discuss." King Nut was furious as he called La'dee's phone, but she didn't answer. The call went straight to voicemail. That only enraged him that much more. The foreman could see his frustration.

"Maybe her phone died. You know women will talk them things dead." King Nut ignored him and headed for his truck. "You should probably try the hotel phone." That stopped him in his tracks and he slowly turned around.

"What hotel?"

"Maybe I'm saying too much, but then again if I were in your shoes, I would expect for someone to do the same for me." The foreman walked up to him and looked King Nut in the eyes a second as if he were reading his very thoughts. "Ms. Walton had me deliver a check to your wife at the Hilton Hotel about thirty minutes ago. And to be honest with you, Mr. Henry, she wasn't there alone. If you know what I mean." King Nut's heart dropped to his stomach and he grew with even more fury. Everything Pay Pay was telling him was proving to be true.

As he rushes off to his truck, the foreman pulls out his phone and dials Pay Pay's phone. "Brad, what's the word?"

"Yeah boss, he just left. I sent him off to the hotel. And that boy was mad enough to bite the head off of a rattlesnake."

"Good. Did you switch his blunt?"

"Yup, I replaced the blunt in his sun visor with the one you gave me."

"Good. He's sure to have a nice trip off that shit. I'll make sure your bonus is in your hands by the end of the night. In the meantime, continue the construction on the club like Ms. Walton requested."

"Will do."

Pay Pay disconnected the call. Just as he pulls to a stop at the streetlights, a tinted out black cargo van skids to a stop in front of him blocking him in. The side door slides open and four men in ski masks hop out with AK-47 pointed at his car. He yanks the gear shift into reverse, but before he could hit the gas, he's hit from behind. A Ford F250 pickup truck had him pinched in.

"Get the fuck out of the car!" one of the men tells him. He was trapped. It was nothing he could do to escape. He just put his hands up and surrendered.

King Dream

Chapter 19

K-Roc and the agents stare down at an empty safe in the closet of the safehouse. "I swear it should've been at least sixteen or seventeen bricks left in here," K-Roc tells agents Mars and Sanders.

"I gave you one day free on these streets to gather all the evidence you can get on King Nut and all you do is lead us to an empty safe?"

"I'm not lying to you, mon. The bricks were here! Me playing no games!"

"Then you better get King Nut on the phone either telling you where those bricks are or admitting he had them or our deal is off!"

"Relax mon. I'll call him," K-Roc says, pulling his phone out. He gets no answer. He calls back a second time and gets an answer on the third ring. "Right now, is not a good time," King Nut says, answering the phone.

"What's the trouble, mon?"

"I'm not in the mood for conversation. I'll talk to you later."

"But this is important." "What is it?"

"The bricks of dope you had in the safe house isn't here. Where did you put them? I have some big orders to fill, mon, and me need some dope."

"What do you mean they're not there!" King Nut was so angry, he didn't even recognize how purposely reckless K-Roc was talking on the phone.

"They're not here. The safe is completely empty mon."
"No dope? No money?"

"Empty!"

"That bomboclat bitch, mon!"

"Who you talk about mon?" King Nut ends the call

without giving him an answer.

"Good job K-Roc. We now got the final nail in King Nut's coffin," Sanders says as he removes the headphones from his head. They had a recording device plugged into K-Roc's cellphone where they were recording and listening in on the call.

"Now what?"

"Now you go back into custody and Audrey goes free. Just like we agreed." Mars nods his head at one of the uniformed officers. The officer walks over and cuffs K-Roc and walks him out to the car.

The squad car transporting K-Roc pulled off from the safe house with Officer Decker behind the wheel and his partner, Officer Reed, riding shotgun.

K-Roc sat handcuffed in the backseat staring out the window trying to rationalize in his mind good enough reasons for setting up King Nut. The only excuse he felt was rational was that he had to look out for Audrey and their unborn child. But even that wasn't a good enough excuse. King Nut was like a blood brother to him and he sold him out. He felt even worse for even trying to justify his snitching. He broke the rules of the game, a rule he swore on his soul a long time ago that he would never break. He couldn't believe how right Mars was when he said everyone has a weak spot.

"Man, Reed, you'll never guess what happened to me last night."

"What?"

"I was working down by MLK street and busted this pretty little blonde for hooking."

"A White girl working Martin Luther King Drive?"
"That's what I said. She stood out like a sore thumb."

"Was she a smackhead?"

"Nope, she wasn't on any drugs."

"If she wasn't on any drugs, then let me guess, she was an undercover?"

"Nope. It turns out she was fresh to the game and her pimp was trying to toughen her skin. So, he put her in the worse area and told her that she couldn't leave the area until she made him five hundred bucks."

"The ole put a whore on the worst track in the city that way when he upgrades her, he could threaten to send her ass back if she fucks up. You got to give it to 'em, these pimps out here are some slick bastards. So, what did you do?"

"What do you think I did? I picked her ass up! Then I pulled into an alley, unzipped my pants, and let her earn the five hundred bucks." Reed and Decker burst out laughing. They were still laughing as their car begin to cross the intersection. Before they got half past the intersection, a bread truck came flying towards them, t-boning them. The crash knocks both Reed and Decker unconscious. K-Roc hits his head on the metal cage divider that divided the front seat from the back. His head was spinning. The men in the bread truck hopped out and surrounded the squad car with their guns drawn. A Tahoe truck pulled up beside the squad car and a couple more men got out. One man opened up the back door of the squad car. K-Roc's head was still spinning, and his vision was blurry. He couldn't make out right away who the men were.

"I know you didn't think the law was going to save yo ass from me, did you?" K-Roc's vision started to come into focus, and he began to see just who the man was standing in front of him. It was Big Folks.

"Me don't look for no mon to save me. Only Jah save mon. And me don't need saving. If you're going to kill me, then go ahead send me to me maker!"

"I'm going to send you there alright, just like I sent yo

boy, Bless. And when I'm done with you, I'm coming for that bitch ass nigga King Nut. But first, I wanted you to watch me send someone else there." Big Folks turns to Boo and nods his head at him. Boo pulls Audrey out of the backseat with her hands bound and mouth gagged. With his gun to her head, she looked petrified. She tries to scream for K-Roc, but her screams were muffled by the gag over her mouth. K-Roc's eyes grew big when he saw they had her.

"Let her go! She has nothing to do with this. This is between me and you, mon! She's pregnant. Leave her out of this!" K-Roc tries to launch out of his seat towards Big Folks. Big Folks kicks him back.

"A man's woman is his rib. They say when a man and a woman have a baby, the two become one. So scientifically speaking, her and that baby she's carrying is a part of you. And I aim to kill everything you stand for." Big Folks ups his .45 and aims it at Audrey's stomach.

"No!!!" K-Roc screams.

BAM! BAM! BAM! BAM!

Officer Reed fires his gun four times, putting two holes into Boo's chest and the other two hit the side of the Tahoe. Audrey runs and hides behind the truck. Decker started to come to just as Big Folks and his boys started shooting at the car. When the bread truck T-boned the squad car, it hit on Decker's side breaking his right leg. With his leg broken and his door smashed in, he couldn't get out of the car. Instead, he got on the radio and called for backup. Reed couldn't get out of the car either with Big Folks shooting at them on his side of the car from beside the Tahoe. Decker, Reed, and K-Roc were sitting ducks because Big Folks and his boys had the squad car surrounded.

They opened up fire on them and bullets riddled the car. Reed catches three shots to the face and slumps over on the steering wheel. Six bullets pierce Decker's chest and he expires. K-Roc catches two to the chest and lays down on the backseat.

The gunshots stopped, and the sirens begin wailing in the distance. Big Folks didn't give a fuck the police were coming. He walks over to the squad car and sees K-Roc laying in the backseat breathing hard with blood covering the front of his shirt.

K-Roc sits up and looks Big Folks square in the eyes with a mean mug on his face. He spits a glob of blood in his face. "Kill me and me see you in the afterlife you Posta Boy!" Big Folks wipes the bloody spit from his face with the hem of his shirt.

"I'll look forward to it."

BAM!

The bullet hit K-Roc square in the head. His eyes rolled into the back of his head and he fell backwards onto the backseat dead. Big Folks put two more into his body to be sure he was dead.

As he turns around, the Tahoe smashes off with Audrey behind the wheel. He points his gun at the truck and squeezes the trigger, but the gun only clicks. He was out of bullets. The other two men shot at the truck but missed. Backup arrived. Squad cars came rushing towards them from all directions. They hop in the bread truck.

The truck's starter wined but wouldn't catch. "Come on bitch, start!" Big Folks turns the key again while pumping the gas and the truck still wouldn't start. The police were getting closer. He tries again and this time it starts up. He quickly puts it into gear and smashes off.

With police on his tail, Big Folks calls Domino. "What up, G?"

"Domino, I got some pigs on my ass. I'm headed south

on Center Street. I'm about to pass the Payless Shoe Store on 12th Street. I need you to pick us up at the Home Depot parking lot."

"I'll be there in eight minutes." Domino ends the call.

Three squad cars catch up to the bread truck. One car rams them from behind. "Get y'all ass back there and get them bitches off our ass!" The two men reload their 223's, open the back door of the truck and begin letting loose on the squad cars. Bullets riddled the windshield of the squad car that was ramming them. The officer behind the wheel slumped over and crashed into a squad car on the side of it. "Hold on!" Big Folks tells them. The men brace themselves as he makes a hard-right turn causing the truck to tilt to the left. The tires on the bread truck screamed as he turned.

They still had another squad car on their ass and more sirens could be heard in the distance. The officer in the passenger seat begins firing shots at them. "Punchy and Lil Larry, I thought I told y'all to get them fags off our ass!"

"We're own it, Folks," Punchy says as he takes aim at the squad car. They squeeze off a round of shots. The police fires back hitting Punchy in the stomach, making him fall out of the truck. The squad car didn't have enough time to swerve around his body and ended up running right over him.

Lil Larry reloads then lays a round of fire on the squad car. Bullets riddled the front end of the car, piercing the radiator and engine causing the police car to stall.

Big Folks makes a left and drives down eight more blocks before hooking another left and abandoning the bread truck. Big Folks and Lil Larry ran across the street to the Home Depot parking lot where Domino was awaiting them. They jump in the Suburban and take off.

"Where the rest of the crew?"

"They didn't make it." Big Folks phone vibrates in his pocket. He pulls it out and sees he has a text message.

"Damn. Did you get that nigga, K-Roc?" Big Folks gave Domino a look that said what the fuck you think. Then he went back to check the message on his phone. "Say no mo. Where you wanna go now?" Big Folks finished reading the message and put the phone away.

"Some lil birdy sent me a text saying King Nut's at the Hilton Hotel downtown." He looks over at Domino. "Get us there."

King Dream

.

160

Chapter 20

La'dee exits the elevator inside the Hilton Hotel and walks down the hall to room 251. She knocks on the door and a few seconds later the door opens. "Ah, La'dee! What a pleasure it is to see you again." La'dee looks strangely at him. "Giorgio, what are you doing here? I was told to meet Paris and Noodles here."

"I invested too and came to collect my cut. Paris asked me to reserve a room here a few hours ago and said she'd be here thirty minutes ago. I called Noodles just a minute ago and she says they're running a little late, but they're on their way. Please, come in and wait with me." La'dee walks in and Giorgio closes the door behind her.

King Nut pulls into the parking lot of the hotel and spots La'dee's car. His heart sank. He couldn't believe what he was seeing. He was hoping that it was all a lie, and it was a valid excuse for everything that was going on. But seeing the video and now seeing her car there in the hotel parking lot, all hope was lost, and his doubts grew even more evident.

He grabs his blunt out of the sun visor and sparks it up. He takes a few hard pulls and sucks the smoke into his lungs and holding it there. As he blows the smoke out, he begins to feel funny. He hears the moans La'dee made in the video playing in his head and he started to hallucinate. A couple standing by a car parked in front of him were kissing. He looks their way, and their faces turn into the faces of Giorgio and La'dee. He shook his head and their faces turned back to normal.

His phone buzzed. He looks down and sees a text message from an unknown caller.

Unknown: Room 251...

He vocally pours his pain out to himself as he loads RIP

bullets into the clip of his .9mm. "Me La'dee, why? Why you do me like this? After all that we've been through. Me wasn't good enough for you? You leave me for another man. A white man. You me wife. 'Til death do we part. Since you want to leave, I'm going to keep me vows and help you depart," he says as he loads the clip into his gun and cocks back the slide to load one into the chamber. He exits the car tucking the gun in the small of his back and pulling his shirt down over it.

"What we did last time ain't going to happen again. Just to let you know. That was a once in a lifetime thing, so, don't get any ideas," La'dee says as she takes a seat on the bed. Giorgio walks over to the bar to prepare a drink.

"La'dee, you were quite the thrill. But you don't have nothing to worry about on that tip. Women are like suits to me. You'll never catch me in the same one twice." His comment made her feel cheap and disposable. She wanted to slap him and give him a piece of her mind, but then her phone rang. She looked at the caller ID and seen it was Noodles calling and answered it right away.

"Noodles, I'm here at the hotel. Where are you?"

"My whereabouts is the least of your troubles right now." Confusion runs across La'dee's face.

"Why you say that?"

"Because King Nut is really pissed off right now." "What for?"

"Let's count the reasons why. One, he found out about your lil affair with Giorgio and your plans to leave him for him. Two, you ripped off the safehouse. And three, you sold his club."

"What? None of that is true! I never ripped off the safehouse, sold the club, or planned to leave me husband."

"That's not what King Nut thinks. You see, we broke off

that safehouse of y'all late last night. Who do you think he's going to blame for that?" Giorgio hands La'dee a drink then turns on some opera music.

"You couldn't have. No one knows where our safe house is."

"I do. You remember that African vase I was checking out at your house. I planted a bug in it and listened for days to all y'all conversations. And when you discussed going to the safe house, I was nearby and followed you when you left out. You lead me right to it. And those papers you just glanced over and signed wasn't to put a lien on the club. It was to transfer the deed over to Paris. If you would've taken the time to read the documents, you would've seen that."

"You bitch. You set me up. Why?"

"It's just business." Someone knocks on the hotel room door. La'dee started to get up to get it, but Giorgio holds a hand up letting her know he got it.

"Nut would never believe this. And when I tell him what you and Pay Pay has done, he'll make sure he's a dead mon. And I'mma kill you myself, you deceitful bitch."

"I don't think your guest at the door is going to give you that opportunity to do so." Noodles ends the call.

BAM!

The shot startled La'dee. She looks towards the door and sees Giorgio's brains spray out the back of his head and his body fall to the floor. As soon as the body fell, she sees King Nut standing in the doorway holding his gun up.

His anger was evident by the expression on his face. His chest pumped up and down as he breathes rapidly. His eyes scanned the scene and he only grew madder. He heard the soft opera music playing and sees the drinks they were sharing. He looks over the way La'dee was dressed in a sexy, short, and revealing peach-colored dress. Flashes of the video of her sleeping with Giorgio played rapidly in his mind. Next thing you know, he blacked out with another hallucination. In the state of hallucination, he sees Giorgio sitting next to La'dee on the bed. He knew he killed him. He looked behind him by the doorway for the body, but sees that his body was no longer lying there. He turns back around, and Giorgio starts talking to him.

"King Nut is it? Well, your majesty, I take it you found out about our little plan to run away together." Giorgio sparks a cigarette. "Now, I know this is hard for you to hear, but La'dee wants a divorce. She needs a real man in her life, that's why she came to me. No need for alimony, we already took everything you got." Giorgio and La'dee bust out laughing. King Nut's face grew grim. He aimed his gun at Giorgio, but Giorgio starts to fade away.

As he was coming out of the hallucination, he could hear La'dee's voice saying, "Nut, I can explain. It's not what it looks -"

BAM! BAM! BAM!

But it was too late. King Nut had squeezed off three shots at Giorgio's ghost, hitting La'dee in the chest. La'dee's body falls backwards onto the bed. King Nut's eyes widen when he realized what he had just done. He dropped the gun and rushed over to her side.

"LA'DEE!" Blood poured from the three holes in her chest.

"Nut, it's not what you think." "Don't talk baby, breathe." "I'm sorry, Nut."

"No, it's me that's sorry. Stay with me, La'dee. I love you, baby, breathe. Just breathe, baby. I'm going to get you some help." La'dee grabs his arm and looks into his eyes.

"I love you too," she says, then she begins shaking and coughing up blood. She was choking on her own blood. King

Nut holds her in his arms and tries to clear her airways, but it was nothing he could do. La'dee had stopped breathing. Tears streamed down his eyes.

"La'dee no!!"

"You called for help," a man says from behind him. King Nut turns around to see a gun pointed at his face.

BOOM!

A 12-gauge sawed-off goes off blasting buckshot into his chest. The shot sends him flying backwards onto the bed. Big Folks walks up to the bed with Lil Larry on one side of him and Domino on the other.

"Bombaclaat."

"This is fo' Big Country, ya bitch."

BOOM! POW! BAM!

King Nut's body jerked as the three of them empty their guns into him. His eyes were wide open, his body was torn and riddled with bullets leaving him without a breath left.

"Long live King Nut," Big Folks says before spitting on his dead body. "Let's get up out of here and head back to the city."

The black pillowcase used to blindfold Pay Pay was removed. Pay Pay adjusted his eyes to the light. He was seated at a table with Joey Long, K-Dolla, and Billy Gunz at the head of the table. Billy Gunz lights up a Cuban cigar with a wooden match. He shakes the match, extinguishing the flame, then tosses it into the ashtray on the table. He leans back in his chair and tilts head up and blows out a cloud of smoke.

"Pay Pay, Pay Pay, you already know what happens when one breaks the laws of the Order. I thought I made myself very clear about not serving Nut or any of my weight in Atlanta," Billy Gunz says.

"That you did. You made yourself crystal clear."

"So, you saying you weren't the one that's been supplying him with bricks?" Joey Long asks him.

"Nah, absolutely I was the one. Nobody else has the balls to serve him."

"Oh, so you deliberately broke the laws of the Order to make some extra bread? Son, don't you know all money ain't good money?" K-Dolla asks. Pay Pay chuckles.

"Y'all think I did this just to make money off this nigga?"

"Then tell us why you put yo life on the line by being his supplier." Billy Gunz stares him down.

"I did it to gain freedom, power, and money." Joey Long and K-Dolla give each other a confused look.

"What do you mean?" Joey Long asks. Pay Pay holds his bound hands up.

"Do you mind?" Joey Long pulls a pocket knife out and cuts the duct tape off his hands. Pay Pay rubs the feeling back into his wrists. "Aight, it's like this. The Order had an issue, and that issue was King Nut. He didn't want to bow down to the Order, so the Order put him on the starve list. Y'all couldn't kill him without running the risk of exposing the Order, so starving him was the best y'all could think to do. Starving him wasn't really working though. He was bullying mothafuckas into buying bad dope from him to stay alive in the game. Starving him wasn't breaking him. The shit was just slowing us down from making money. Y'all put me in a predicament where I had all this dope and couldn't even hustle it in my own city. Something had to change and sitting back waiting for King Nut to crack wasn't going to do it. So, like a true hustla that I am, I took matters into my own hands. After serving Big Country a few times when me and Noodles first started coming down here to Atlanta, I found out he was an informant for the FEDs. If I was going to take over the city, I had to get rid of him first. But I knew if I did it myself, Big Folks and his disciples would rain more hell on me than I could handle on my own, so I had King Nut do it. It was a chess move. I knew Big Folks would find out he did it and come for him. And if Big Folks killed him, it wouldn't bring any exposure to the Order. In the midst of all this, Noodles and Paris hustled his wife out of fifty G's, their club, and over seventeen bricks."

"It sounded like a good plan. Too bad it ain't work," Joey Long says.

"How come it didn't?"

"Last we checked King Nut was still alive."

"Oh yeah? I think you'd betta check again, pimp." Billy Gunz's phone rings. He picks it and puts it on speakerphone.

"Yeah."

"Billy G, this Big Folks." "What's good, Big Folks?"

"I was just letting you know my business down in the A is complete. Me and the G's are headed back to the city as we speak."

"You found that peace you were looking for?" "You betta believe I did."

"Good. Take care, bruh, and be smooth." "Always." Big Folks disconnects the call. "Didn't I tell you?" Pay Pay says.

Billy Gunz blows out a puff of smoke and looks at him with a stern face. He stands up and slowly claps his hands. Joey Long and K-Dolla joins in.

"Congratulations, lil brother. You passed the test," K-Dolla says.

"Test?"

"Yeah, we put you in that predicament on purpose. We could've easily got rid of King Nut, but we wanted to see if you were going to be content with those current hustle arrangements or if you were going to rise up and prove

167

yaself as a real hustla. You did that and did it brilliantly," Billy Gunz tells him.

"You made us proud, baby boy," Joey Long says.

"Does this mean I make it to the next level?" Billy Gunz cracks a slight smile.

"You'd betta believe it."

TO BE CONTINUED...
Nightmares of a Hustla 3
Coming Soon

Submission Guideline

Submit the first three chapters of your completed manuscript to ldpsubmissions@gmail.com, subject line: Your book's title. The manuscript must be in a .doc file and sent as an attachment. Document should be in Times New Roman, double spaced and in size 12 font. Also, provide your synopsis and full contact information. If sending multiple submissions, they must each be in a separate email.

Have a story but no way to send it electronically? You can still submit to LDP/Ca$h Presents. Send in the first three chapters, written or typed, of your completed manuscript to:

LDP: Submissions Dept
Po Box 944
Stockbridge, Ga 30281

DO NOT send original manuscript. Must be a duplicate.

Provide your synopsis and a cover letter containing your full contact information.

Thanks for considering LDP and Ca$h Presents.

Coming Soon from Lock Down Publications/Ca$h Presents

BOW DOWN TO MY GANGSTA

By **Ca$h**

TORN BETWEEN TWO

By **Coffee**

THE STREETS STAINED MY SOUL **II**

By **Marcellus Allen**

BLOOD OF A BOSS **VI**

SHADOWS OF THE GAME II

By **Askari**

LOYAL TO THE GAME **IV**

By **T.J. & Jelissa**

IF LOVING YOU IS WRONG... **III**

By **Jelissa**

TRUE SAVAGE **VIII**

MIDNIGHT CARTEL III

DOPE BOY MAGIC IV

CITY OF KINGZ II

By **Chris Green**

BLAST FOR ME **III**

A SAVAGE DOPEBOY III

CUTTHROAT MAFIA III

DUFFLE BAG CARTEL VI

By **Ghost**

A HUSTLER'S DECEIT III

KILL ZONE **II**

BAE BELONGS TO ME III

A DOPE BOY'S QUEEN III

By **Aryanna**

COKE KINGS V

KING OF THE TRAP II

By **T.J. Edwards**

GORILLAZ IN THE BAY V

3X KRAZY II

De'Kari

THE STREETS ARE CALLING II

Duquie Wilson

KINGPIN KILLAZ IV

STREET KINGS III

PAID IN BLOOD III

CARTEL KILLAZ IV

DOPE GODS III

Hood Rich

SINS OF A HUSTLA II

ASAD

KINGZ OF THE GAME VI

Playa Ray

SLAUGHTER GANG IV

RUTHLESS HEART IV

By Willie Slaughter

THE HEART OF A SAVAGE III

By Jibril Williams

FUK SHYT II

By Blakk Diamond
TRAP GOD III
By Troublesome
YAYO IV
GHOST MOB
Stilloan Robinson
KINGPIN DREAMS III
By Paper Boi Rari
CREAM II
By Yolanda Moore
SON OF A DOPE FIEND III
By Renta
FOREVER GANGSTA II
GLOCKS ON SATIN SHEETS III
By Adrian Dulan
LOYALTY AIN'T PROMISED III
By Keith Williams
THE PRICE YOU PAY FOR LOVE II
By Destiny Skai
CONFESSIONS OF A GANGSTA III
By Nicholas Lock
I'M NOTHING WITHOUT HIS LOVE II
SINS OF A THUG II
By Monet Dragun
LIFE OF A SAVAGE IV
MURDA SEASON IV
GANGLAND CARTEL III

By **Romell Tukes**
QUIET MONEY IV
THUG LIFE II
By **Trai'Quan**
THE STREETS MADE ME III
By **Larry D. Wright**
THE ULTIMATE SACRIFICE VI
IF YOU CROSS ME ONCE II
ANGEL III
By **Anthony Fields**
FRIEND OR FOE III
By **Mimi**
SAVAGE STORMS II
By **Meesha**
BLOOD ON THE MONEY III
By J-Blunt
THE STREETS WILL NEVER CLOSE II
By K'ajji
NIGHTMARES OF A HUSTLA III
By King Dream
THE WIFEY I USED TO BE II
By Nicole Goosby
IN THE ARM OF HIS BOSS
By Jamila
MONEY, MURDER & MEMORIES II
Malik D. Rice

Available Now

RESTRAINING ORDER **I & II**
By **CA$H & Coffee**
LOVE KNOWS NO BOUNDARIES **I II & III**
By **Coffee**
RAISED AS A GOON I, II, III & IV
BRED BY THE SLUMS I, II, III
BLAST FOR ME I & II
ROTTEN TO THE CORE I II III
A BRONX TALE I, II, III
DUFFLE BAG CARTEL I II III IV V
HEARTLESS GOON I II III IV
A SAVAGE DOPEBOY I II
HEARTLESS GOON I II III
DRUG LORDS I II III
CUTTHROAT MAFIA I II
By **Ghost**
LAY IT DOWN **I & II**
LAST OF A DYING BREED
BLOOD STAINS OF A SHOTTA I & II III
By **Jamaica**
LOYAL TO THE GAME I II III
LIFE OF SIN I, II III
By **TJ & Jelissa**
BLOODY COMMAS I & II

SKI MASK CARTEL I II & III

KING OF NEW YORK I II,III IV V

RISE TO POWER I II III

COKE KINGS I II III IV

BORN HEARTLESS I II III IV

KING OF THE TRAP

By **T.J. Edwards**

IF LOVING HIM IS WRONG...I & II

LOVE ME EVEN WHEN IT HURTS I II III

By **Jelissa**

WHEN THE STREETS CLAP BACK I & II III

THE HEART OF A SAVAGE I II

By **Jibril Williams**

A DISTINGUISHED THUG STOLE MY HEART I II & III

LOVE SHOULDN'T HURT I II III IV

RENEGADE BOYS I II III IV

PAID IN KARMA I II III

SAVAGE STORMS

By **Meesha**

A GANGSTER'S CODE I &, II III

A GANGSTER'S SYN I II III

THE SAVAGE LIFE I II III

CHAINED TO THE STREETS I II III

BLOOD ON THE MONEY I II

By J-Blunt

PUSH IT TO THE LIMIT

By **Bre' Hayes**

King Dream

BLOOD OF A BOSS **I, II, III, IV, V**
SHADOWS OF THE GAME
By **Askari**
THE STREETS BLEED MURDER **I, II & III**
THE HEART OF A GANGSTA I II& III
By **Jerry Jackson**
CUM FOR ME I II III IV V VI
An **LDP Erotica Collaboration**
BRIDE OF A HUSTLA **I II & II**
THE FETTI GIRLS **I, II& III**
CORRUPTED BY A GANGSTA I, II III, IV
BLINDED BY HIS LOVE
THE PRICE YOU PAY FOR LOVE
DOPE GIRL MAGIC I II III
By **Destiny Skai**
WHEN A GOOD GIRL GOES BAD
By **Adrienne**
THE COST OF LOYALTY I II III
By Kweli
A GANGSTER'S REVENGE **I II III & IV**
THE BOSS MAN'S DAUGHTERS I II III IV V
A SAVAGE LOVE **I & II**
BAE BELONGS TO ME I II
A HUSTLER'S DECEIT I, II, III
WHAT BAD BITCHES DO I, II, III
SOUL OF A MONSTER I II III
KILL ZONE

176

A DOPE BOY'S QUEEN I II

By **Aryanna**

A KINGPIN'S AMBITON

A KINGPIN'S AMBITION **II**

I MURDER FOR THE DOUGH

By **Ambitious**

TRUE SAVAGE I II III IV V VI VII

DOPE BOY MAGIC I, II, III

MIDNIGHT CARTEL I II

CITY OF KINGZ

By **Chris Green**

A DOPEBOY'S PRAYER

By **Eddie "Wolf" Lee**

THE KING CARTEL **I, II & III**

By **Frank Gresham**

THESE NIGGAS AIN'T LOYAL **I, II & III**

By **Nikki Tee**

GANGSTA SHYT **I II &III**

By **CATO**

THE ULTIMATE BETRAYAL

By **Phoenix**

BOSS'N UP **I , II & III**

By **Royal Nicole**

I LOVE YOU TO DEATH

By Destiny J

I RIDE FOR MY HITTA

I STILL RIDE FOR MY HITTA

King Dream

By **Misty Holt**
LOVE & CHASIN' PAPER
By **Qay Crockett**
TO DIE IN VAIN
SINS OF A HUSTLA
By **ASAD**
BROOKLYN HUSTLAZ
By **Boogsy Morina**
BROOKLYN ON LOCK I & II
By **Sonovia**
GANGSTA CITY
By **Teddy Duke**
A DRUG KING AND HIS DIAMOND I & II III
A DOPEMAN'S RICHES
HER MAN, MINE'S TOO I, II
CASH MONEY HO'S
THE WIFEY I USED TO BE
By Nicole Goosby
TRAPHOUSE KING **I II & III**
KINGPIN KILLAZ I II III
STREET KINGS I II
PAID IN BLOOD **I II**
CARTEL KILLAZ I II III
DOPE GODS I II
By **Hood Rich**
LIPSTICK KILLAH **I, II, III**
CRIME OF PASSION I II & III

178

FRIEND OR FOE I II

By **Mimi**

STEADY MOBBN' **I, II, III**

THE STREETS STAINED MY SOUL

By **Marcellus Allen**

WHO SHOT YA **I, II, III**

SON OF A DOPE FIEND I II

Renta

GORILLAZ IN THE BAY **I II III IV**

TEARS OF A GANGSTA I II

3X KRAZY

DE'KARI

TRIGGADALE I II III

Elijah R. Freeman

GOD BLESS THE TRAPPERS I, II, III

THESE SCANDALOUS STREETS I, II, III

FEAR MY GANGSTA I, II, III IV, V

THESE STREETS DON'T LOVE NOBODY I, II

BURY ME A G I, II, III, IV, V

A GANGSTA'S EMPIRE I, II, III, IV

THE DOPEMAN'S BODYGAURD I II

THE REALEST KILLAZ I II III

Tranay Adams

THE STREETS ARE CALLING

Duquie Wilson

MARRIED TO A BOSS... I II III

By Destiny Skai & Chris Green

KINGZ OF THE GAME I II III IV V

Playa Ray

SLAUGHTER GANG I II III

RUTHLESS HEART I II III

By Willie Slaughter

FUK SHYT

By Blakk Diamond

DON'T F#CK WITH MY HEART I II

By Linnea

ADDICTED TO THE DRAMA I II III

IN THE ARM OF HIS BOSS II

By Jamila

YAYO I II III

A SHOOTER'S AMBITION I II

By S. Allen

TRAP GOD I II

By Troublesome

FOREVER GANGSTA

GLOCKS ON SATIN SHEETS I II

By Adrian Dulan

TOE TAGZ I II III

By Ah'Million

KINGPIN DREAMS I II

By Paper Boi Rari

CONFESSIONS OF A GANGSTA I II

By Nicholas Lock

I'M NOTHING WITHOUT HIS LOVE

SINS OF A THUG
By Monet Dragun
CAUGHT UP IN THE LIFE I II III
By Robert Baptiste
NEW TO MONEY, MURDER & MEMORIES
THE GAME I II III
By **Malik D. Rice**
LIFE OF A SAVAGE I II III
A GANGSTA'S QUR'AN I II III
MURDA SEASON I II III
GANGLAND CARTEL I II
By **Romell Tukes**
LOYALTY AIN'T PROMISED I II
By Keith Williams
QUIET MONEY I II III
THUG LIFE
By **Trai'Quan**
THE STREETS MADE ME I II
By **Larry D. Wright**
THE ULTIMATE SACRIFICE I, II, III, IV, V
KHADIFI
IF YOU CROSS ME ONCE
ANGEL I II
By **Anthony Fields**
THE LIFE OF A HOOD STAR
By Ca$h & Rashia Wilson
THE STREETS WILL NEVER CLOSE

By K'ajji

CREAM

By Yolanda Moore

NIGHTMARES OF A HUSTLA I II

By King Dream

BOOKS BY LDP'S CEO, CA$H

TRUST IN NO MAN

TRUST IN NO MAN 2

TRUST IN NO MAN 3

BONDED BY BLOOD

SHORTY GOT A THUG

THUGS CRY

THUGS CRY 2

THUGS CRY 3

TRUST NO BITCH

TRUST NO BITCH 2

TRUST NO BITCH 3

TIL MY CASKET DROPS

RESTRAINING ORDER

RESTRAINING ORDER 2

IN LOVE WITH A CONVICT

LIFE OF A HOOD STAR

King Dream

CPSIA information can be obtained
at www.ICGtesting.com
Printed in the USA
LVHW051706190421
684911LV00011B/1401